Escape to the Dales

Also by Bob Allen

ON HIGH LAKELAND FELLS   ON FOOT IN SNOWDONIA   WALKING THE RIDGES OF LAKELAND
ON LOWER LAKELAND FELLS   SHORT WALKS IN THE LAKE DISTRICT   WALKING MORE RIDGES OF LAKELAND

Looking north up Wharfedale, with Yockenthwaite Moor on the skyline

ESCAPE TO THE DALES

45 Walks in and around the Yorkshire Dales

Bob Allen

A MERMAID BOOK

MICHAEL JOSEPH LTD

Published by the Penguin Group
27 Wrights Lane, London W8 5TZ
Viking Penguin Inc., 375 Hudson Street, New York, New York 10014, USA
Penguin Books Australia Ltd, Ringwood, Victoria, Australia
Penguin Books Canada Ltd, 10 Alcorn Avenue, Toronto, Ontario, Canada M4V 3B2
Penguin Books (NZ) Ltd, 182–190 Wairau Road, Auckland 10, New Zealand

Penguin Books Ltd, Registered Offices: Harmondsworth, Middlesex, England

First published in Great Britain April 1992
First published in Mermaid Books (with revisions) June 1996

1 3 5 7 9 10 8 6 4 2

Copyright © Bob Allen 1992, 1996

Typeset in 11/12 pt Goudy Old Style
Printed in Singapore by Imago Publishing

A CIP catalogue record for this book is available from the British Library

ISBN 0 7181 3510 5

The moral right of the author has been asserted

Illustration on page 1: The western Howgills seen from Seat Knott

CONTENTS

Introduction   page 7
Glossary   12
Acknowledgements   13

Part 1: Ribblesdale and Dentdale
1. Catrigg Force and Attermire Scar   17
2. The Round of Crummackdale   21
3. Ingleborough and Gaping Gill   25
4. Ingleton Glens and Twisleton Scars   29
5. Ingleborough and Raven Scar   33
6. The Round of Kingsdale   37
7. Ease Gill and Great Coum   41
8. Whernside from Dent   45
9. Over Rise Hill, Dentdale   49
10. Birkwith and Alum Pot   53
11. Pen-y-ghent and Plover Hill   57
12. The Three Peaks Walk   61
13. Smearsett, Pot and Giggleswick Scars   69
14. Fountains Fell and Malham Tarn   73

Part 2: The Howgills, Baugh Fell and Mallerstang
15. Yarlside and the Eastern Howgills   79
16. Cautley Spout and The Calf   83
17. Baugh Fell: The Waterfalls Walk   87
18. Round of the Western Howgills   91
19. Carlin Gill and Black Force   95
20. The Langdale Skyline   99
21. Mallerstang: The Crest and the Edge   103
22. The Nine Standards and Whitsundale   107

23. Swarth Fell and Wild Boar Fell   111
24. Grisedale, Hell Gill and the High Way   115

Part 3: Wensleydale and Swaledale
25. Aysgarth Falls and Penhill   121
26. Waldendale and Harland Hill   125
27. Drumaldrace from Marsett   129
28. Addlebrough and the Devil's Stone   133
29. Askrigg's Waterfalls and Beyond   137
30. Pike Hill from Hawes   141
31. The Swale Gorge and Swinner Gill   145
32. Gunnerside Gill and the Lead Mines   149

Part 4: Wharfedale, Littondale and Nidderdale
33. Malham Cove and Gordale Scar   155
34. Posforth Gill and Simon's Seat   159
35. The Western Skyline of Barden Moor   163
36. The Wharfe and Trollers Gill   167
37. Grassington's Old Lead Mines   171
38. Grassington to Kettlewell   175
39. The Monk's Road   179
40. The Littondale Skyline   183
41. Buckden Pike via Buckden Beck   187
42. The Head of Wharfedale   191
43. Over Old Cote Moor   195
44. Great Whernside and Dowber Gill   199
45. How Stean Gorge and the Head of
     Nidderdale   203
Index   206

INTRODUCTION

It is many years since my own first real introduction to the Dales – through a dustbin lid into a hole in the ground in Kingsdale. Within a few minutes I was in a narrow passage, water to my waist and then to my chin, my helmet scraping the roof above and one ear under water. It was my initiation to potholing, but after a year or two of standing around on a freezing moor trying to get my sodden things off and then get warm again, I decided that walking the fells on top suited me better than going underneath them.

I've done almost all these walks again over the last eighteen months and they represent my choice of the best.

There are many reasons for buying and owning a guide-book to walks, especially if it has attractive photographs or illustrations, but they seldom include taking it with you on the walk itself. If I like the look of a walk from the pictures and illustrations, and all the other relevant detail such as distance, time, terrain, degree of challenge etc appeals, I then try to follow the walk on the relevant map, making either mental or written notes and sometimes highlighting the map with a fluorescent marker-pen. Obviously, it is then sensible to take the map on the walk, particularly in an unfamiliar area.

The walks in this book are all selected from the 800-odd square miles of what I might call the Greater Yorkshire Dales National Park, for I have included Mallerstang, the Howgills (half of which are in the main National Park) and the head of Nidderdale as well.

Within this area is a tremendous variety: bleak, high and lonely gritstone moors, home to grouse and curlew; fascinating former leadmines around Swaledale and Grassington; marvellous patterns of fields and walls with isolated farmsteads and delightful villages nestling in the valley bottoms below brilliant white limestone scars (or cliffs). For those not familiar with the northern landscape, I have included a glossary of words used to describe its features.

It is wonderful walking country, but without some help or foreknowledge it can be frustrating too. Many of the right of way paths are those which linked settlements in an age before people walked, as now, for pleasure and recreation. These paths sometimes avoid natural lines and features such as ridges and gills which are attractive to modern walkers but new paths and tracks are being added, sometimes as permissive

Traditional Dales barn and pasture in Upper Wharfedale

The cliffs of the Swale Gorge and the Old Beldi mine workings seen from the fields behind Keld

paths across obvious farmland (a process in which the National Park authorities play a vital part) and at other times simply by walkers pressing for further access, for the freedom to roam. Many walkers have come across the signs that say bluntly and irritatingly 'No Road' – but without pointing out where the 'road' is. On the other hand, many landowners realize that the vast majority of walkers do respect the life of the countryside, take pains to do no damage and therefore turn a blind eye to what may be technically trespasses. It is easy enough to go astray and I have done so myself but I do make it a matter of honour never to knock the stones off walls – or to replace them immediately if I do – and always close gates. In selecting the walks in this book, I have tried to stay as closely as possible to rights of way and established permissive paths but if I have got it wrong anywhere and you are challenged by a landowner, please retire gracefully and don't argue 'But it says in this book . . .' because that will only make matters worse. One of my golden rules is that if I knock a stone off accidentally, I will *always* replace it. I urge you to do the same and to respect the landowners over whose property you are walking.

Overall star rating: The 'star rating' at the beginning of each walk is completely subjective but I hope it will give some clue as to the overall quality – i.e. fine scenery, variety of interest etc – of each walk. I should point out that a walk that may only get one star is still very well worth doing; there are many other walks that I don't consider to be worth one star at all and they have not been mentioned.

Distances: Those given are calculated from the map, not from paces on the ground. My distance for the Three Peaks Walk, for example, could be as much as two more miles when allowance is made for the rise and fall of the land covered.

Heights: The highest elevation reached is the summit or highest point on the walk. On the other hand, the height gained will take some account of any descent and re-ascent that may be made during the course of the walk. For example, the walk over Old Cote Moor crosses and re-crosses the moor and so the height gain is almost double that in just going up to the highest point. The actual heights given for summits do vary slightly on OS maps from one edition

Scale Force in Hebden Gill

9

to another and from one type of map to another – e.g. Great Coum is given as 686m on my edition of the 1:50,000 scale map but as 687m on the 1:25,000 scale.

Times: Perhaps with an eye to the fact that many walkers in the Dales don't get a move on quite as they would in Scotland or on the high fells of Lakeland, perhaps because there are many stiles to cross, I have allowed an average of about two miles per hour for these walks, though most walkers comfortably exceed that when they are actually walking. In practice, this two miles an hour should allow enough time for short stops.

Maps: I give grid references for most suggested parking places and occasionally to help locate other places: therefore, readers unfamiliar with the grid system should look at any OS map where it is always described. A magnetic compass is rarely essential but it is very useful and I make frequent reference to heading north or south-west and so on (as well as left and right) in the directions which will, I hope, avoid confusion.

The OS 1:50,000 scale Landranger 98 *Wensleydale and Upper Wharfedale* map covers many of the walks in this book and may be perfectly adequate, especially when walking on the higher land where the features are natural rather than man-made, but the 1:25,000 scale Outdoor Leisure maps to the Yorkshire Dales numbers 2 (*Western area*), 10 (*Southern area*) and 30

(*Northern & Central areas*) are excellent and particularly useful in the limestone areas of the Dales because walls are normally shown. (A wall, however, may prove to be a collapsed line of stones or a wire fence when you actually get there.) Nevertheless, walking in the valley bottoms, or escaping from them to the higher land, can be much easier if you can pinpoint your exact position. I hate messing about with two maps on a walk: in wind or rain it can be enough of a trial coping with one, so I have tended to choose as 'best map' the single one which, from my experience on the ground, covers the walk most successfully. I should add that I have also always used the maps which I have found readily on sale in the area.

My own maps are drawn on an approximate scale of 1:50,000, just to draw attention to the key features of any particular walk and to put it in its geographical context. I have put contour lines on almost all the maps where they may help to define the general shape of the landscape, but not otherwise. The walks are marked with red broken lines and arrows, but where the walk goes along a well-marked track (e.g. a walled but unmetalled lane) I have used a solid red line.

For the Howgills area, where navigation is perfectly simple in good visibility but can be very tricky in bad, I have differentiated between the type of cairn found on the summits, because whether it is an OS trig point, a large and well-built cairn or a little pile of stones on the top of the relevant summit can be an additional help in defining one's position.

I actually used the 1:25,000 Pathfinder sheets

The end of Twisleton Scar, with Kingsdale and Gragareth beyond

NY 60/70 (*Tebay and Kirkby Stephen*) and sheet 69/79 (*Sedbergh and Baugh Fell*), but have since discovered, used and can strongly recommend the Harvey Mountain Map *Howgill Fells, Cumbria* which is drawn on a 1:40,000 scale (1½″ = 1 mile). This shows all the Howgills as well as Baugh Fell and Wild Boar Fell on one map and, what is more, it is printed on waterproof paper too. Where this, as a single map, covers the area of the walk, that is the one I have recommended as the best.

Apart from the normal booksellers and specialist outdoor equipment suppliers, maps are usually on sale at the Yorkshire Dales National Park Information Centres at Sedbergh, Aysgarth Falls, Clapham, Grassington, Hawes and Malham; note, however, that in winter they only open at weekends.

11

GLOSSARY

Erratics. This is a geological term used to denote boulders or stones being found in a place where they might not normally be expected – i.e. limestone blocks on top of gritstone moorland. The movement of ancient glaciers and their subsequent melting and deposition of the debris they were carrying usually explains their presence.

Gates. This means 'road' or 'path', the word deriving from the Scandinavian 'gatan' of the same meaning – i.e. Kirkby Gate.

Ginnel. A narrow passage way, often between buildings.

Green ways. These are ancient trackways, often grass-covered and sometimes walled: they often give delightful walking.

Groughs. These are exclusively found on the gritstone moors and are the channels or grooves cut by rainwater in the surrounding peat. The areas of peat left surrounded by the groughs are the 'hags'.

Intake wall. This is (usually) the last wall up the fellside: beyond it is more open pasture or moorland.

Neb. This refers to a jutting high point of land; like a nose or the peak of a cap.

Nicks. On limestone, the passage of feet, even over many years, leaves little impression and so there are places in the limestone Dales where nicks, which are cuttings or grooves, were hacked out of the rock of a skyline so that a traveller could align with them even in misty weather and not lose his way – i.e. Kirkby Nick.

Pavements, clints and grikes. Exposed areas of limestone are usually known as 'pavements', which is what they resemble; the best of them are very dramatic indeed. The action of surface rainwater eats away at the pavement and carves it into blocks or clints. The channels are known as grikes or grykes and often provide a site for delicate plants like the harts-tongue fern, where they are protected from the sheep.

Shake hole. Sometimes known also as 'swallet-holes' or 'swallow-holes'. These are depressions in the ground, rather like tunnel-shaped craters and are found in limestone country where water has drained through the permeable limestone and may well indicate the surface opening of vast underground cave systems. Shake-holes may develop into potholes and some of them have delicately-fluted sides of great beauty.

ACKNOWLEDGEMENTS

I must acknowledge the great help of my old friend Reg Atkins since over the years he has suggested a number of the walks in this book, ones which we have done together. Trevor Jones and Diana McIlreavy have accompanied me on walks, in the Howgills especially; and my two little canine pals, Henry the Second and Freddie, have been great company on the walks in all weathers.

My debt to the wonderful maps of the Ordnance Survey is incalculable, for I have pored over them for hours working out possibilities.

Mike Harding's lovely book *Walking the Dales* will be known and loved by many and his lyrical writing and humorous enthusiasm certainly inspired me to look more closely at a few areas I thought I already knew, for many of the most interesting finds in the Dales are hidden away, rarely so obviously on show as in the Lake District. Gladys Sellers' book *The Yorkshire Dales – A Walker's Guide to the National Park* is a mine of interesting information and ideas; Reg and Alice Hainsworth of Ingleton lent me their copy of *The Three Peaks of Yorkshire* by Harry Ree and Caroline Forbes, which I found very illuminating; John Hardy's book *The Hidden Side of Swaledale* extended my insight into the lead mining era; Geoffrey Wright's book on *Roads and Trackways of the Yorkshire Dales* deepened my overall background knowledge, while the much-loved (and now sadly passed) A. Wainwright's *Walks in Limestone Country* is a classic, still a little gem and likely to remain so.

Finally, but by no means least, my debt to my editor, Jenny Dereham, is immense; she has queried every little inconsistency, forced me to see every walk from the point of view of somebody who knows nothing about the area at all and has consequently made the whole book much more valuable to every reader.

I hope my photographs will give pleasure to those who do know the area and, to those who don't, some inspiration to go and visit it.

View over High Winskill and Ribblesdale to Smearsett and Pot Scars

PART ONE

Ribblesdale and Dentdale

1.   Catrigg Force and Attermire Scar

Best map: OS 1:25,000 Yorkshire Dales (Western area)

Distance: About 7 miles/11.2km

Highest elevation reached: 1197ft/365m

Height gained: 705ft/215m

Overall star rating: * *

General level of exertion needed: Low/medium

Time for the round: About 4 hours

Terrain: Mostly on green lanes and paths; quite a few stiles.

This walk is a very worthwhile expedition with a great variety of attractive limestone scenery.

Park in the delightful little town of Settle, usually busy, but try near the viaduct first (grid ref. 819638). From the left-hand side of the market square, opposite the famous 'Ye Olde Naked Man Café' (though his effigy on the wall clearly shows three things looking like buttons up the front of his chest), climb up Constitution Hill, past terrace houses, bending left then levelling out, and take the first rough walled lane on the right beyond the bend. This climbs to a gate and sloping sheep pasture. Now contour at this level towards Langcliffe by keeping close to the left-hand wall, entering and leaving more walled lane, climbing a ladder-stile on the left, crossing an enclosed field and continuing above a clump of trees, to curve downhill to Langcliffe village. This has many Restoration buildings, a spacious green, a fine hall and a huge sycamore tree with a *semi*-circular bench (which Jim Hacobian told me was an example of Yorkshire canniness). This same bard of Langcliffe (he's now written over fifteen hundred sonnets) most generously insisted on our first meeting that I take with me a bag full of home-made cakes and biscuits.

Go down the lane opposite the green (second right after entering the village); this lane becomes walled and you should follow it until it ends at two field gates. Directly ahead now is the impressive cliff of Langcliffe Quarry, and a green way beyond the right-hand gate goes along the top side of the field ahead. Beyond another gate, it climbs steadily to the right of the cliff to reach higher pastures and to a ladder-stile on the left, beside a walled lane. Go over this and across the field to another, then right towards the hamlet of Upper Winskill. Here is a welcome finger-post: 'Catrigg Force ⅓', so now follow the open path, via two stiles and a large field, down towards a clump of trees into which a stream drains from

Approaching Langcliffe Quarry, Ribblesdale

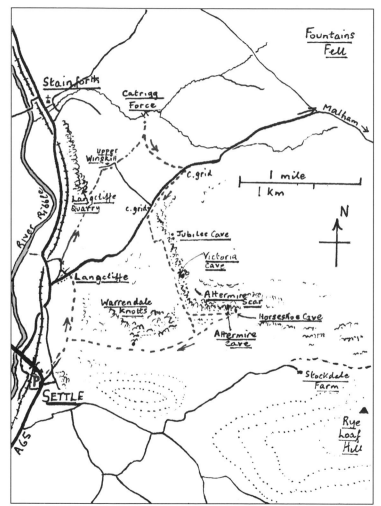

Fountains Fell. Here the waters of Catrigg Force, the finest in the Craven District, take a double leap into a lovely rocky hall adorned with mature trees. From here, an obvious path leads quickly down to the lower level.

On returning to the stile at the top of the large field, bear left (south-east) on a track leading to a cattle-grid at the Langcliffe to Malham Moor road (grid ref. 839666), then continue south-west along this to another (grid ref. 835659). Turn left here (footpath sign), uphill, on a green way below limestone scars on the left to a stile, then go left again towards higher land and climb another stile beyond which the twin entrances of the not especially interesting Jubilee Cave are visible almost directly ahead. Continue southwards, with a pap-like hill very prominent on the skyline ahead, keep left over a stile (signed 'F.P. Stockdale Lane 1½'), along a path below more limestone scars at the left side of a U-shaped valley until it curves up to the enormous entrance to Victoria Cave. This was discovered in 1837 but was greatly enlarged after its importance was realised. Remains of rhinoceros and hippopotamus were eventually unearthed at the lowest levels excavated; Neolithic Man left flints and a stone axe and even later occupants left beads, coins, brooches, pottery and iron weapons.

The path continues below the escarpment (Attermire Scar) and, as the Scar swings left and becomes higher and steeper, descends slightly to a gateway where a sign 'Settle 1½' points west along a green

Evening light on Attermire Scar

pathway. This leads below the steep outcrops of Warrendale Knotts, past a little cave at the foot of a rocky ridge, over the rise and down the field to meet the outward route.

For a more adventurous finish to the day, however, rather than descending to the gateway take a rising path on the left along a terrace directly underneath Attermire's main crags. The great vertical cave at the end, partly blocked by a chockstone, is Horseshoe Cave; the real Attermire Cave is higher up. To find the latter, go back fifty paces to a little black hole and Attermire Cave is thirty feet directly above it; however, it is best reached by going back a further fifty paces, scrambling up easy ground onto the next terrace and walking right. This time it is unmistakable: a classic, keyhole-shaped entrance becoming a narrow tube. When I visited the cave, I crawled for what seemed miles, but when I had only three of my wind-proof matches left I lost my nerve; I believe I would have entered a larger chamber with a pool. Back outside again, descend grassy scree to the gateway in the pastures and the way home.

2.   The Round of Crummackdale

Best map: OS 1:25,000 Yorkshire Dales (Western
    area). Also on OS 1:50,000 Landranger 98
    (Wensleydale and Upper Wharfedale)

Distance: About 7½ miles/12km

Highest elevation reached: 1345ft/410m

Height gained: 846ft/258m

Overall star rating: * * *

General level of exertion needed: Medium

Time for the round: About 4 hours

Terrain: Mostly on grass paths or splendid
    limestone clints.

This walk is a fine, natural and complete circuit of Crummackdale's skyline over some of the region's finest limestone pavements; you visit the famous Norber 'erratic boulders' and continue round the head of Crummackdale over Moughton. The views are splendid, the walking delightful.

Austwick is a charming village, just off the busy A65 main road, with a green, a church, a restored cross, a comfortable inn and many attractive cottages. The most convenient parking for this walk is at grid ref. 769692: take the Horton road, turn up Townhead Lane and, at the top of a rise, it crosses a track with a sign 'BW Clapham 1½ FP Norber ½' where there is space for a few cars.

Go left (west) along the track a few paces, then take the 'Norber' stile. Robin Proctor's Scar (named after a farmer who jumped down it on his horse after a visit to the pub; his horse was killed but he apparently survived) is on the left as you cross a field to a wall and continue alongside it, not through the gate, to another stile in a wall-corner. Climb the slope beyond and then northwards towards the plateau, veering right onto a large sloping sheep pasture. Here the famous Norber erratics are scattered around, boulders of dark Silurian rock, carried along by the retreating glacier and deposited on this limestone shelf. The limestone weathers faster and consequently some of the dark boulders are perched on plinths of white limestone, a curious sight.

Now climb up and across the field to a ladder-stile, and a slanting line upwards soon lands you on a limestone pavement, with excellent views up Crummackdale. The limestone escarpments all around the head of the valley are now clearly visible and show the continuing line of the walk. Climb to the highest tier – there are various cairns though no obvious paths – and Ingleborough comes into view. Keep heading

From the clints near Norber looking along Crummackdale

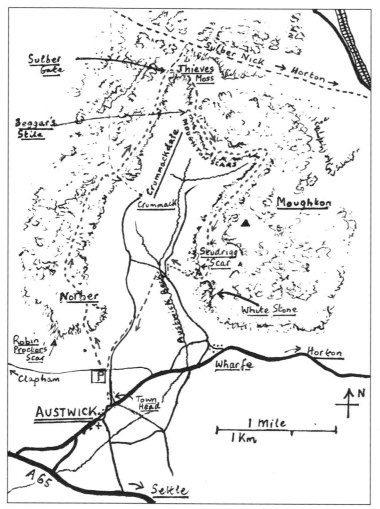

north between the rocky tiers, making for the gleaming white horizontal line of pavement (Moughton Scars), with the distinctive shape of Pen-y-ghent directly behind it. Cross a green way and a track from Austwick to Horton and then, beyond a little neb topped by intensely green grass, meet a wall rising from Crummackdale. Don't try climbing it for you quickly reach Sulber Gate (gate and stile in a wall-corner).

Here take the small wicket-gate on the right which leads down onto the grassy bit called, for some reason lost in the mists of time, Thieves Moss. You are now on the great pavement between the upper and lower tier of Moughton Scars. At one place, flakes of limestone are jammed vertically between the clints like teeth, very tightly wedged, and just beyond is Beggar's Stile at the little breach in the escarpment where a path descends to Crummackdale; however, go left along the edge of the scar overlooking Crummackdale. A neb of jutting crags follows, leading round a side valley and then you start to climb gently up towards Moughton, the edge softening as you pass through a zone of dwarf juniper bushes. The sketchy path stays on the higher level, curving away from the sharp edge of Studrigg Scar (not visible from up here), by-passing the trig point on the summit of Moughton itself, then fades away into sheep tracks.

A large cairn (grid ref. 783708) is an obvious objective, standing out on a rounded headland, and just beyond it is a shallow, dry valley trending towards Crummackdale, with a wall running across it. Follow

*Towards Moughton
Scars with Pen-y-ghent
on the skyline*

the line of this wall south-east across this dry valley and, fifty yards before the wall itself ends at the top of the steep crags of White Stone, use a through-stone stile to cross the wall. Now descend, trending sharply right to where a waterfall used to pour over the lip of the scar, terminating the dry valley above. The water appears lower down the scree, draining towards a field corner and gate, with another gate beside sycamore trees just beyond.

Go through this gate into a walled lane (towards the village of Wharfe) but at the first junction turn right on another lane leading to a ford and slate-slab footbridge over the Austwick Beck. Over the bridge take the ladder-stile on the left and go south-west up the field, over the next stile and down the field on the other side to reach the wall-corner where a tarmac track leads to Sowerthwaite Farm. Ahead is a gate and cattle-grid; turn left down the minor walled road just beyond and follow it downhill, curving round the end of Norber towards Robin Proctor's Scar again and in five minutes you are back at the parking spot just outside Austwick.

3. Ingleborough and Gaping Gill

Best map: OS 1:25,000 Yorkshire Dales (Western area). Also on OS 1:50,000 Landranger 98 (Wensleydale & Upper Wharfedale)

Distance: About 11 miles/17.6km

Highest elevation reached: 2372ft/723m

Height gained: 1857ft/566m

Overall star rating: ***

General level of exertion needed: Medium/high

Time for the round: About 5½ hours

Terrain: On good paths, though often boggy on the high gritstone moorland and they are faint on the limestone after the first part of the descent.

Ingleborough is essentially an 800-ft thick plinth of limestone, capped by a cone of repeated layers of shales, other limestones and sandstones (the Yoredale Series) and a thin, impervious gritstone layer on top. Water drains down to the limestone, carves potholes, passages and caves on the way and then reappears at the base of the plinth. Probably the best-known pothole of all is Gaping Gill, reputed to be big enough to easily absorb St Paul's Cathedral, but this is only one of about a hundred such potholes descending into this truly hollow mountain. This route to the top has more variety than any other: it is the best, the classic way.

Park in Clapham where there is a very good National Park car park at grid ref. 745692. Turn right on leaving it, cross over the packhorse bridge, turn right, left at the corner ahead, then go through the farm gate on the right and pay a small fee to walk the well-kept paths through the delightful Ingleborough Estate. Pass an attractive (man-made) lake fed by Clapham Beck, with ornamental trees, plants and shrubs, many of which were planted by Reginald Farrer, most renowned of a distinguished (and somewhat eccentric) family; other members built a 200-yard long tunnel for use by the servants so that they wouldn't be seen by the owners or their guests when coming from the village to the Hall.

The path steepens near the end of the lake, passes a folly, the Grotto, and, leaving the woods, passes the entrance to the very impressive Ingleborough (show) Cave, hard by whose entrance is the Beck Head resurgence where the waters that disappear down Gaping Gill reappear. From here, Clapdale is a classic dry limestone valley; the route turns left into the imposing, narrowing and vertical-sided Trow Gill,

Gaping Gill and Ingleborough

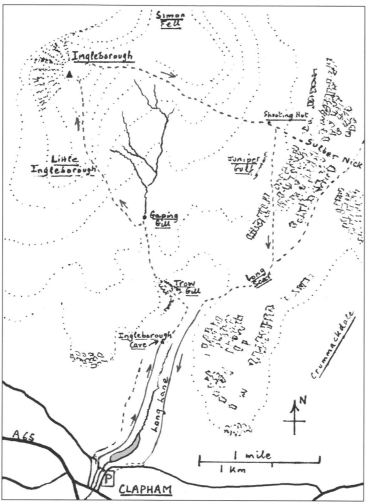

where the path emerges from a slot at the far end of the gorge into a twisting grassy valley with a wall alongside. Ignore the first stile on the left; the second leads over the wall to a swallow-hole and Bar Pot, the normal entrance for cavers into the Gaping Gill system. To reach Gaping Gill, don't cross that stile either but keep on over some peaty moor to reach the fence surrounding it; here the Fell Beck plunges about 340 feet (twice the height of Niagara Falls) in Britain's longest unbroken waterfall, though in the dark, of course.

A broad and usually soggy path now climbs north-west towards a bold cairn on the top of Little Ingleborough, then a level section follows before a final steep haul to the summit plateau with its wide-ranging views, archaeological remains and sheep.

The descent starts from the north-east corner of the plateau where the well-worn Three Peaks path sets off towards Horton in Ribblesdale, heading east off the main ridge and very boggily across the flank of Simon Fell. It descends steadily and then almost on the level to a ruined shooting-hut (grid ref. 767740). Take care here, for navigation can be tricky as you have reached a huge expanse of level limestone pavement and the eroded tracks on the peat almost disappear on the rock. Ahead is a stile in the wall and if it's clear weather this is a good moment to turn right along the wall to have a look for Juniper Cave and, just to its right, Juniper Gulf, a maze of ostensibly harmless crevices below which apparently lurk great crevasses.

Return to and cross the stile, then at the first finger-post past the shooting-hut another faint path goes south (not east) over an expanse of clints and grikes to join an old droving way at Long Scar, thence going south-west round the hillside to a gate and the end of the (walled) Long Lane: Trow Gill is over the wall, down in the dip on the right.

However, if you fail to spot this faint path south (which just cuts a corner anyway), keep on eastwards, as signed, to a single finger-post (grid ref. 778735) marked 'Clapham'. Turn right here – or you'll end up in Horton – and follow the track to Sulber Gate and, keeping right so as to avoid dropping down to Crummackdale, you will reach Long Scar and Long Lane as above.

In the walled lane you can't go wrong. It joins Thwaite Lane where you turn right and pop through the tunnels under Ingleborough Hall to emerge near the church again in Clapham at the end of a most satisfying day.

Whernside seen from the summit plateau on Ingleborough

27

4.   Ingleton Glens and Twisleton Scars

Best map: OS 1:25,000 Yorkshire Dales (Western
    area). Also on OS Landranger 98
    (Wensleydale & Upper Wharfedale)

Distance: About 8 miles/12.9km

Highest elevation reached: 1280ft/390m

Height gained: 754ft/230m

Overall star rating: * * *

General level of exertion needed: Medium

Time for the round: About 4–5 hours

Terrain: Good paths through the Glens, then on
    grass and limestone pavement.

The 'Glens and Waterfalls Walk' of Ingleton, with its profusion of gorges, wooded ravines, sparkling waterfalls and deep pools, is perhaps the best of its type in the British Isles and justifiably popular. For years I kept away, put off by the thought of hordes of people and that I would have to pay parking-cum-entrance fee for enduring them. Well, it's worth every new penny! Choose a day in the middle of the week or go in winter, and it is surely unbeatable value. However 4¼ miles is hardly a good day out for a self-respecting fellwalker so, unless you've only a couple of hours to spare, extend it to take in the fine limestone pavements of Twisleton Scars as well and it becomes a really good round.

The 'Waterfalls' are signed on the approach roads in Ingleton and there is a huge car park (grid ref. 693734) just beyond the impressive ex-railway viaduct spanning the ravine where two rivers meet. Eminent writers such as Wainwright and Harry Ree have disagreed about their names: I'll stick with the Ordnance Survey and call the western one the Twiss and the eastern the Doe. After their confluence they are called the Greta.

The walk starts up the Twiss, up the wooded Swilla Glen, on an excellent footpath, until the valley narrows and a footbridge leads across to the other bank, shortly returning by way of another bridge. This is just below some old quarries where vertical slates of blue Ingletonian rock are in sharp contrast to the nearby white limestone and from where the roar of rushing water can clearly be heard. Ahead can be seen the Pecca Falls, followed by one of the Twin Pecca Falls. Climbing out of the ravine, the path heads across pasture, curving right to reveal a wide basin into which pours the most impressive Thornton Force; here the water thunders over a horizontal limestone lip which is supported on an undercut lump

Thornton Force, Ingleton

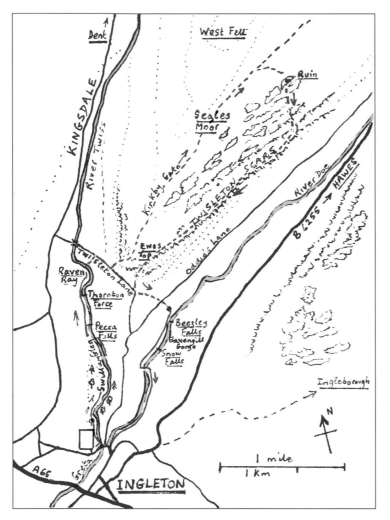

of vertical slate. It is an exciting place, and it is easy and usually safe to scramble behind the waterfall to look through the curtain of water and just wonder at the colossal forces which turned one lot of rocks vertically on end and left another lot horizontal on top of them. The path climbs now to the left of the waterfall to Raven Ray, the limestone valley above, where debris left by the great glacier that carved out Kingsdale once formed a barrier that the river now cuts through. A footbridge leads across the Twiss, enabling the path to join Twisleton Lane.

Turn right along the lane to reach the gate with the iron kissing-gate beside it, then climb steeply up to the left just beyond it on the green way of the Kirkby Gate. Follow the Gate towards the scars above and then up the broad back of the ridge until you pass through a sort of cutting in the ridge-top – the Kirkby Nick – and reach Ewes Top. This bit is just the same as in Walk 6. From here, however, do not follow the nearby wall (which leads eventually to the top of Whernside) but stay with this ancient packhorse track from Ingleton to Ribblehead leading north-east over a grassy moorland plateau, Scales Moor, at about the same height for a couple of miles. You'll pass the occasional incipient pothole with elegantly fluted sides, and then clints will reappear. The path is sometimes rather vague but keep well below the ridge with its wall and stay on a north-easterly course until you spot a ruined sheepfold to the right (south-east) amidst a field of limestone boulders (grid ref. 727777). Go due south from here to a large conical cairn which proves to be almost on the cliff top of Twisleton Scars overlooking the valley of the River Doe. The cliff top provides the line of a splendid return walk, with a wall as an additional guide, all the way back to Twisleton Lane. Here you have signs pointing down the field and across the old Roman road of Oddie's Lane to Beezleys Farm and so forward to Beezley Falls.

I once walked along Oddie's Lane from Chapel-le-Dale on a dark winter's night when a car flashed past doing at least sixty mph. Within a few yards, I found a huge hare in the road, quite dead but still twitching. Being partial to roast hare, I picked it up and carried it home. When I presented it to my wife, however, she screamed and nearly threw me out. You might have thought it was a mouse!

An excellent path now follows the course of the Doe as it snakes down the ravine, past the thunderous Baxengill Gorge to Snow Falls and then crosses over to the east bank. Here it climbs away from the gorge and finally rambles gently back to the centre of Ingleton. A wonderful outing!

Pecca Twin Falls, Ingleton

5. Ingleborough and Raven Scar

Best map: OS 1:25,000 Yorkshire Dales (Western area). Also on OS 1:50,000 Landranger 98 (Wensleydale & Upper Wharfedale)

Distance: About 8½ miles/13.6km

Highest elevation reached: 2372ft/723m

Height gained: 1844ft/562m

Overall star rating: **/***

General level of exertion needed: Medium/high

Time for the round: About 4–5 hours

Terrain: Stony track, peaty moorland, limestone clints – in that order.

Ingleborough from Ingleton is the most direct way up this fine mountain and a good round is made by descending to Raven Scar on the west flank and then walking back along the extensive limestone pavements found there.

The start of the walk (grid ref. 702731) is directly opposite Storrs Hall Bungalow, just up the B6255 to Hawes at the edge of the town. Park on the common (space for about ten cars) at the very end of Fell Lane, or in little roadside quarries just beyond. An 'Ingleborough' finger-post will point up the common to where Fell Lane becomes walled at the top of the first rise and from here you get your first brief sight of the mountain. The walls end at a gate, then the track crosses open pasture, round a curve and there's the delightful farm of Crina Bottom, nestling between limestone scars and surrounded by trees. It's a fine example of the way you can sometimes stumble upon surprise views in the Dales that you would never suspect from a distance.

The way ahead is obvious enough now, up three separate tiers beyond the farm. First, there is a stretch of peaty moorland whose underlying rocks are clearly not limestone but bands of shale, sandstone and mudstone which make up the Yoredale Series. A second tier, of limestone, follows, forming a collar round the mountain and although this is not too obvious as you toil upwards, it becomes much more so as you reach the final tier, a layer of millstone grit about a hundred feet thick, which is above it. I find it fascinating to think that this mountain top was once submerged beneath the delta of a great river flowing over West Yorkshire to the sea.

As you pull onto the great plateau on top, the OS trig. point is only a few yards away, as are several cairns, a four-sided windbreak, a view indicator, the ruins of a military wall and foundations of circular

Approaching Ingleborough from just beyond Crina Bottom

33

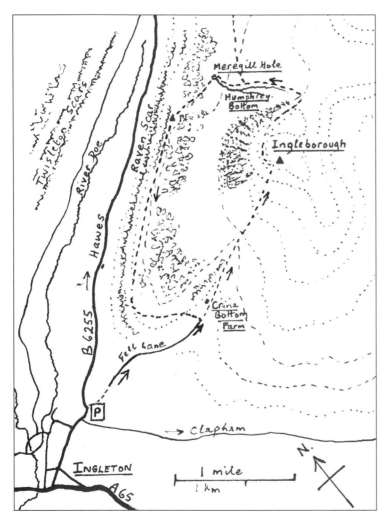

huts: in fact, it is probably the most interesting summit in the British Isles in this respect, for it was the site of a hill-fort probably built by the Brigantes against the Romans.

From the northern edge of the summit plateau a path leads east, quickly descending to a lower level where a long curve of fellside with a sharply defined edge makes a great sweep to the north-east; from here there are fine views across to Whernside and to the happily saved Ribblehead Viaduct on Batty Moss. One path continues along the edge but a steeper one should be taken which leads down almost immediately, northwards towards Humphrey Bottom. This is well used by the Three Peaks walkers and care is needed in descending its mixture of rock, rubble, mud and earth down what is soon seen as the line of Mere Gill. Reaching the moor, bear left (north-east) along the line of the gill, away from the main path, to the second clump of rowans; here a stile in the wall on the left gives access to the unmistakable pothole of Meregill Hole.

The limestone layer has been reached again and the stream promptly disappears down the pot, though some of it can be seen again down a fissure lower down the fellside. Potholers regularly try a through-passage here but a key passage often fills with water so they are also regularly defeated.

Due west on the skyline are a square stone shooting-butt and a tall cairn, giving new objectives along the vast pavements of Raven Scar which form a plinth for the mass of Ingleborough. Passing the

34

From Raven Scar with Twisleton Scars in mid-distance and Gragareth on the skyline

remains of Harry Hallam's sheepfold, the way is slightly uphill to the big cairn, which is four-sided and about ten feet high, and then on towards more cairns to the south-west. The way passes over alternate rocky and grassy stretches, with fine views over to Twisleton Scars and to Gragareth's skyline. Along this stretch, I once watched a weasel with his black-tipped tail leap off a clint and disappear down a grike, then reappear chasing a rabbit. My dogs saw them and joined in, weasel and rabbit both vanished and two confused dogs, to my amusement, wondered where they'd gone.

Eventually a solitary tree appears on the skyline to the right of another cairn and beyond this the land slopes downhill more noticeably to reach a wide, grassy shelf just above Crina Bottom. A green way snakes down here, through the escarpments above the farm. A transverse wall is soon reached and, as you turn left along the wall, you are quickly at the gate at the end of Fell Lane which leads back to the car.

6.   The Round of Kingsdale

Best map: OS 1:25,000 Yorkshire Dales (Western area). Also on OS 1:50,000 Landranger 98 (Wensleydale & Upper Wharfedale)

Distance: About 13 miles/20.9km

Highest elevation reached: 2415ft/736m

Height gained: 2090ft/637m

Overall star rating: **

General level of exertion needed: Medium/high

Time for the round: About 6 hours

Terrain: Grassy paths to Whernside; rough moorland then easy to Gragareth; steep descent but grassy return along the Turbary Road.

Whernside is the highest hill in the Yorkshire Dales National Park, thus worth climbing even if it were just a heap of rubble. On a good day, however, its ascent from the south-west by West Fell can be a grand expedition with far-ranging views from its summit. To return along the other ridge of Kingsdale is a chance to tramp along the boundary of the Park, visiting Gragareth (which, apart from its famous Three Men of stone on its flank, is hardly worth a visit on its own despite its resounding name), then descend to the Turbary Road for a most interesting final stage. You should take a torch for visiting Yordas Cave.

There is parking for a few cars at the south end of Kingsdale where Twisleton Lane leaves the Thornton in Lonsdale to Dent road (grid ref. 692760); or in a layby on a bend slightly towards Thornton. Now go down Twisleton Lane, over the footbridge and along to the gate with the iron kissing-gate beside it; then just beyond it climb steeply up to the left on the green way (grassy track) called the Kirkby Gate. Follow the Gate towards the scars above and then up the broad back of the ridge until you pass through a sort of cutting in the limestone, the Kirkby Nick, and reach Ewes Top. Now leave the Kirkby Gate, which continues over Scales Moor to Ribblehead, and trend left to shadow the wall which points straight as an arrow up the distant ridge to Whernside. Imperceptibly, limestone changes to gritstone as you start to climb West Fell. You then join the much-used Three Peaks path along a stretch of it which has been drained and channelled. One last stile and there is only a short trudge to the top.

Leave the trig point by descending due west on a fair path towards Kingsdale, to a gritstone edge with four cairns close together, then turn sharply right to

Looking up Kingsdale; Whernside is on the right-hand skyline

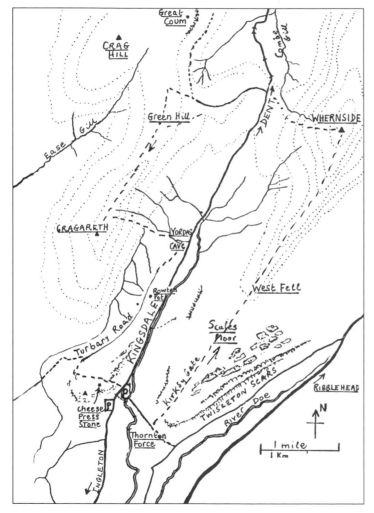

meet a wall, then turn downhill to reach the Dent road. On the descent you can see the old walled track of the Occupation Road contouring round the hillside at a higher level, and the aim now is to follow this generally westwards and then proceed beside the fence and broken wall over rough ground directly up to the ridge-top. There's a wall along the top and it is just a tramp along a broad peaty ridge, sometimes with views as far as the Lake District beyond Ease Gill.

The trig point on the summit is well to the west of the wall but there's a ladder-stile leading over it just north of the trig point, and another wall leads from here directly down steep slopes to the south-east, making straight for a clump of trees which is where Yordas Cave, formerly a show cave, is hidden in the ravine. The entrance to the cave is near the foot of the gill, down some steps leading to a man-made stone archway. You will need your torch to get a glimpse of an impressive cascade pouring down into a circular chamber seen through a natural arch.

On leaving the cave, turn right and slant uphill towards two small escarpments and a gate, and you are then on the Turbary Road which runs along a natural limestone shelf. This was the right of way for the peat-cutters; it is also the level at which the waters draining from Gragareth meet the permeable limestone and sink into it, forming a multitude of potholes and caverns below your feet, and reappearing in a resurgence at Keld Head lower down the valley, a deep pool much used by cave-divers. Rowan trees often indicate potholes and Jingling Pot is to be found near some to the right, but you will easily spot the tremendous chasm of Rowten Pot next to the path just beyond the second gate; this hole is unfenced and very dangerous. A few yards further south, the much smaller pot has a plumb drop of 235 ft.

There are more but less obvious potholes, but it is delightful walking along this green and grassy way, with a few more gates, until it begins to swing away from Kingsdale, approaching the only clump of trees just off to the right of the track. Here you pass through a gateway in a wall running SSW in exactly the direction you need and, as you follow it downhill, you're bound to notice a large isolated square block of stone on the skyline to the right. This is the Cheese Press Stone, probably dumped there by the retreating glacier as it is so relatively unscarred. The sketchy path goes slightly to one side of it before winding down more steeply over a little escarpment to a final ladder-stile. Just beyond is the road and the parking place at Twisleton Lane again.

*Rowten Pot beside the
Turbary Road, Kingsdale*

39

7.   Ease Gill and Great Coum

Best maps: No one map covers the area. The OS
    1:25,000 Yorkshire Dales (Western area) has
    all except the start and finish. OS 1:50,000
    Landrangers 97 (Kendal to Morecambe) and
    98 (Wensleydale & Upper Wharfedale)
    between them cover the whole walk

Distance: About 8½ miles/13.6km

Highest elevation reached: 2254ft/687m

Height gained: 1677ft/511m

Overall star rating: **/***

General level of exertion needed: High/medium

Time for the round: About 4–5 hours

Terrain: Paths to Bullpot Farm and the start of
    Ease Gill, then rough gorge-walking and
    mostly open moorland for the remainder.

This is a superb walk of great contrasts, between the extraordinary close-up scenery of the limestone section of Ease Gill and the wild gritstone fells, with their far-ranging views, beyond.

The start is in Barbondale which links Dentdale to the little village of Barbon which is just off the A683 between Kirkby Lonsdale and Sedbergh. From Barbon village, take the Dent road up Barbondale (where I always seem to see pheasants perched on the walls) to a point just before the road bends left and crosses a stream from the right (Aygill Beck) at grid ref. 655826. There are numerous parking spots just off the road.

Now take the rough track heading south-east, initially up the line of Aygill until that curves away left onto the open moor, then over the rise, through a gate to a walled lane leading directly to the end of the road from Casterton to Bullpot Farm; the latter is now a centre for caving. Go south now, immediately left of the farm buildings, down a path which soon passes a big fenced-off pothole on the right, which engulfs the stream; this is 'Bullpot of the Witches'. Reach a stile with signs for 'Lancaster and Cow Pots', and 'Hellot Scales Barn, Ease Gill'. The path threads between an extraordinary number of shake-holes before reaching the slowly crumbling barn set on a bank just above the dry bed of Ease Gill. Don't go down into the ravine yet or you will miss some of the most interesting sights; instead, keep going down the tongue of land between Ease Gill and another gill on the right. Quite suddenly and dramatically the right-hand gill is full of water: this is the Leck Head resurgence where all the waters draining from Leck Fell are forced again to the

*Towards Ingleborough
from Great Coum*

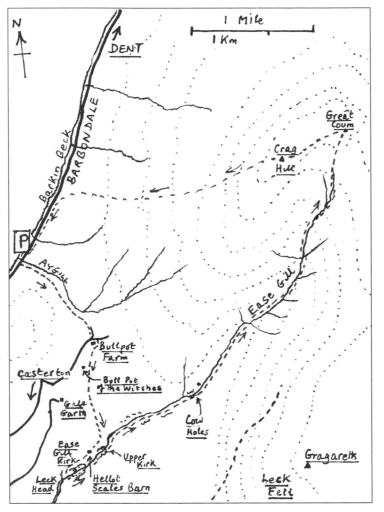

surface as they meet impermeable rocks and go flooding away down the valley to join the River Lune.

Turn left now up Ease Gill itself. If you choose the left bank, you can cross the fence and descend to the ravine beyond a deep pool, rather like walking round part of the lip of a cauldron. Either bank leads into the great and impressive rock hall of Ease Gill Kirk where the water has cut through the limestone at its far end, leaving a polished lip halfway down. A pile of stones beyond a pool shows where attempts are made to scale this lip into the upper kirk, but if there's any water coming over the lip it will probably be too slippery and you'll have to retreat out of the gill to one side.

A little further up the ravine, beyond Hellot Scales Barn, will be found another version of the kirk: a deep chamber with a U-shaped outlet and numerous basin-shaped pools whose rocky sides are highly polished by the scouring action of the water. My dog Henry slithered into one and had to be rescued: the more he splashed and scrabbled, the more slippery the sides became.

Follow the course of the gill upstream, to the point where a side stream enters from the left, leaving the bed of the gill ahead virtually dry. In front can be seen another deep defile and the sound but no sight — although you are obviously in the stream-bed — of a tumbling waterfall. It is rather eerie and, as you approach and peer round the corner, there's a deep boomerang-shaped pool where the water swirls, gurgles and vanishes at your very feet; this is fed by a cascade coming over a double-lipped chamber at the far end. This most impressive place is Cow Hole, or Cow Dubs.

Climbing out into the gill above, you find a wall and a bridge and then Oxford Pot below an iron cover a little further up the left bank. Now the valley becomes wider and more open and you can see the eminence of Great Coum a long way ahead on the skyline. Just keep on now up the line of the main stream as it becomes more of a ravine again. Pass a fine little waterfall with a natural limestone slab bridging the stream below (known as a 'God's bridge') and work your way uphill, with plenty of rough going, until the stream vanishes in a bog. It's now only a short pull to the wall and cairn on Great Coum, a broad flat top but with fine views over Dentdale: to Rise Hill, Baugh Fell, Ingleborough, Whernside and the Howgills.

To return, you could descend to the north to pick up the old rutted way of the Occupation Road, follow it round to Barbondale and along the grassy verge back to the parking area or, the way I prefer, go west to the OS cairn on Crag Hill and then choose your own line down the west flank of Barbon High Fell to reach Barkin Beck much lower down the valley.

Ease Gill Kirk

8.   Whernside from Dent

Best map: OS 1:25,000 Yorkshire Dales (Western area). Also on OS 1:50,000 Landranger 98 (Wensleydale & Upper Wharfedale)

Distance: About 12½ miles/20km

Highest elevation reached: 2415ft/736m

Height gained: 1975ft/602m

Overall star rating: * *

General level of exertion needed: Medium/high

Time for the round: About 5–6 hours

Terrain: Some easy walking but plenty of open fell and rough ground.

This is arguably the best way up Yorkshire's highest mountain, which is at the head of one of Yorkshire's loveliest dales; the walk has plenty of variety and some wonderful views.

The start is in the quaint and lovingly-preserved village of Dent which retains a stretch of echoing cobbles and some delightful old houses. If you use the car park at grid ref. 704872, walk eastwards a few steps along the main road to the cobbled section: here one almost expects a cry of 'Gardeyloo!' and to have to dodge a bucket of slops. Then take the right fork (not the Hawes road) and fork right again in fifty paces to find an initially metalled but soon rough lane winding up the wooded Flinter Gill. Little waterfalls are heard here but not easily seen. Continue steeply upwards to where the lane emerges as a rutted track joining another contouring the wide slopes of Great Coum. This track is called the 'Occupation Road' and is marked on the OS map as 'Green Lane (Track)'. It is an old packhorse road, probably from Ingleton to Lancaster, which was walled about 1859 as the higher fells were increasingly enclosed and 'occupied'. In places, particularly further on, it is just like walled bog where the old culverts that took the water from streams crossing its line have been damaged, but in others it is a fine highway. The polished black limestone known as 'Dent marble' – seen in Bradford's Cartwright Hall and elsewhere – was quarried along here, as well as at Arten Gill which is, of course, crossed by one of the famous viaducts on the Settle to Carlisle railway line.

Not far along the track and visible on the fellside above is a group of 'stone men', the Megger Stones, large cairns erected by nameless men for an unknown and somewhat puzzling purpose. Their magic seems to evaporate as you reach them, but from a distance they do excite curiosity and a sort of wonder. Although it's

Looking down Deepdale from near the top of the Occupation Road

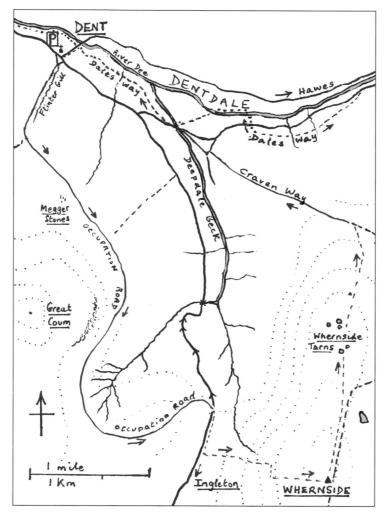

a bit of a climb and off-route a little, I can never resist making the effort for a closer look.

Carefully following the contours, the Occupation Road curves round to the east, giving a splendid view down Deepdale to Dentdale, and finally meets the motor road making its spectacular descent from Kingsdale to Dent. Here it is necessary to walk up the road, but only for a couple of hundred yards until, on the far side of the wall descending from Whernside, the path is clearly seen leading up the fellside. This is the bit that does you good: uphill work for a mile, alongside the wall until it reaches a little escarpment, swinging right to a group of cairns and then up again to the top. Compared with the paths up Whernside from the Ribblehead side, this one has no erosion problem: it's more like a rabbit track and if you keep on the trig point side of the wall as you head north off the summit towards Whernside Tarns, you will be hardly aware of the battered track on the other side. To be fair though, a great deal of work has been done to improve this – drainage channels dug and sections of unsightly but effective duck-boarding put in place.

When the main ascent path veers off to the north-east on its way back to Ribblehead, keep heading north to pass Whernside Tarns, sometimes little more than puddles surrounded by mud, and at other times quite large sheets of water; a distinct cairn beyond them is a guide ahead. This is just where the ground shelves steeply down to Deepdale in the west, but easier slopes lead to the north-east and going down this way enables a junction to be made with the

fine old green track of the Craven Way, soon becoming walled in places and giving easy walking down towards the junction of Deepdale and Dentdale.

Reaching the valley bottom, the old track runs close by Whernside Manor which used to be the home of the National Park Cave and Fell Centre but is now an outdoor adventure centre for the Army. (When you keep meeting lads abseiling to attention in the Lakes or Dales nowadays, you know they're either from Catterick or Whernside Manor.) From here on, it's just the last little bit of Dyke Hall Lane to meet the road at the corner by the Deepdale Methodist Chapel, down the road to Mill Bridge over Deepdale Beck and a last ramble alongside the beck on the Dales Way into Dent. Here I can recommend the Stone Close Café for an excellent tea.

The Megger Stones above Dentdale

9. Over Rise Hill, Dentdale

Best map: OS 1:25,000 Yorkshire Dales (Western area). Also on OS 1:50,000 Landranger 98 (Wensleydale & Upper Wharfedale)

Distance: About 12 miles/19.2km

Highest elevation reached: 1824ft/556m

Height gained: 1388ft/423m

Overall star rating: */**

General level of exertion needed: Medium

Time for the round: About 5½–6 hours

Terrain: Mostly over grass and sheep tracks on the ascent and traverse of the ridge. The return along the Dales Way from Cowgill to Dent is on good paths, inevitably with many stiles.

This was an enjoyable tramp along the high ridge-top separating Dentdale from Garsdale, with some fine views to the Howgills, Garsdale and the amazing high-level line taken across the fells by the Settle to Carlisle railway.

A wonderful late afternoon glow on Rise Hill, seen on several occasions from Great Coum and Whern-side, tempted me to seek a walk here. There is a path on to the west end of the ridge, beyond is obviously high moorland at the same sort of altitude as the great mass of Baugh Fell on the other side of Garsdale. I could not imagine that I was the first to spot such an obviously fine ridge and so felt fairly confident that I would find a path along it and a descent that would give few problems. I couldn't be absolutely sure for paths are continually changing, being re-aligned or created; even the OS maps can be out of date. When my old friend John Forder admitted that he had not yet walked the length of the ridge on his own doorstep, despite having lived in Dent with his wife Eliza for a dozen years and having crawled down every passage and pothole under every fell for miles around, I saw the opportunity for some companionship as well.

It was on a bright November morning that we left Dent (the car park is at grid ref. 704872) and walked the short distance north-westwards along the road to where it runs next to the River Dee. There is a signed path to Barth Bridge which we crossed. Following the road for a hundred paces along the north bank brought us to a minor tarmac road leading up Blea Beck Gill and, staying on the tarmac strip all the way, got us quickly to Lunds Farm and a rough walled lane beyond the farm buildings. This ends at a sheepfold,

The Howgills and Garsdale from the cairn on Aye Gill Pike

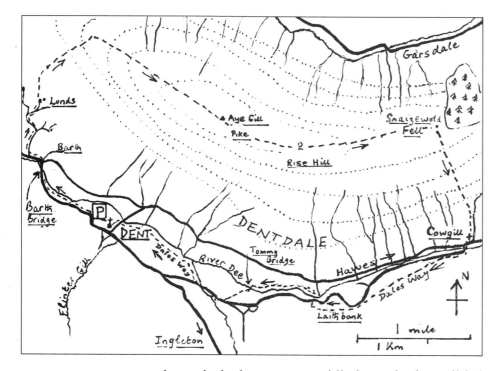

years, and we soon reached the trig point on Aye Gill Pike. There are old workings up here, quarrying perhaps, and a fine tall cairn a little further along the ridge and down the slope; it's a splendid place from which to view Garsdale.

Now a long descent beside the wall over the rest of Rise Hill, with Great Knoutberry Hill and Wold Fell in view all the way, led us to the much brighter green grass-covered limestone pavement on Snaizewold Fell. Here we sat and watched a train on its way south from Carlisle curving round the opposite fellside, appearing and disappearing as it went from tunnel to cutting to viaduct (Artengill and Dent Head Viaducts are both visible from up here) until it vanished into Blea Moor Tunnel.

I can't be precise about getting down from the fell-top and you might think of better ways – for instance, by continuing a little further east to join the lane that runs down to Cowgill. We simply climbed carefully back to the Dentdale side of the ridge-top wall and headed approximately south-east. I remember we had one more wall to cross, by big through-stones, and we crawled through a large hogget-hole (big enough for humans as well as sheep) to join the walled lane and so down to Cowgill. Here we emerged next to St John's Church, turned right down the road and almost immediately crossed the bridge over the Dee, where the water flows over sculpted limestone slabs.

Finding the path of the Dales Way was easy enough for, after just a little walking along the road, it was

beyond which open grassy fell alongside the wall led us upwards – perspiring heavily, for it was much warmer than the early frost had led us to expect and we were in sunshine now – to reach the main wall running the length of the fell. A careful climb over this to the Garsdale side disclosed a grand view of the Howgills, the great hump of Baugh Fell and the steady trudge ahead of us. There was a sketchy path, many of the walls on the Garsdale side have been collapsed for

*On the descent to
Cowgill from Rise Hill,
with Artengill Viaduct*

signed on the left: 'F.P. Laithbank 1¼'. We didn't get any more sun that day because our path was in the shadow of Whernside and Great Coum, but it glowed on Rise Hill while we climbed stiles in and out of two lots of conifer plantations and across pastures, all marked and signed to 'Laithbank'. Here we turned down the track to the road again and after a short walk along this took the footpath on the right signed to 'Lenny's Leap'. Neither of us knows what that is but it leads to a footbridge and the other bank, and then a pleasant walk as far as Tommy Bridge. Here we found it advisable to cross back to the southern bank and follow the 'Dales Way' signs back to the village. It had been a grand day.

10. Birkwith and Alum Pot

Best map: OS 1:25,000 Yorkshire Dales (Western area)

Distance: About 10½ miles/16.8km

Highest elevation reached: 1165ft/355m

Height gained: 403ft/123m

Overall star rating: */**

General level of exertion needed: Low

Time for the round: About 4½–5 hours

Terrain: A roughish lane at the start but then almost all on good paths.

This is an almost level walk along the grassy limestone shelves above both banks of the upper waters of the River Ribble. The wide views over the rolling moors are much better than one might expect and the secret gills, caves and potholes add fascinating variety.

Start from the car park in Horton in Ribblesdale (grid ref. 807726), cross the main road and go up Harber Scar Lane just to the right of The Crown hotel. This is part of the Pennine Way, an old packhorse route to Hawes and after about twenty minutes of stony plod, interest is quickened by the sound of a rushing beck on the right; however, it promptly dives down the deep main pot of Sell Gill Holes immediately beside the track – the other one, though dry, is on the other side. The main pot is reckoned to be about 200 feet deep and its huge chamber is apparently only second in size to the main chamber of Gaping Gill.

Leave the Pennine Way at the gate ahead and go left to pass Sell Gill Barn (finger-post to Birkwith) and then, with the wall on the left, keep on along a wide green way just below extensive low scars. This is easy and delightful walking below the scars but above the line of farmsteads, passing a ruined chimney (an industrial relic) and over the odd stile, until a long open field ends abruptly at a fairly shallow gill (grid ref. 804766), the first since Sell Gill; here cross the wall in its bottom via the stile. Just beyond is a much deeper and more heavily wooded ravine, Birkwith Gill, fenced off but easily accessible by turning right uphill beside the fence and curving round the head of the gill (with Old Ing Farm now in view) to a stile, beyond which is a good view of the wide horizontal slot of Birkwith Cave. Here the waters rush out impressively into a deep fissure at right-angles to the slot and then turn again down the ravine.

Now pick up the track from Old Ing down to High

Winter in Upper Ribblesdale; from Selside to Pen-y-ghent

53

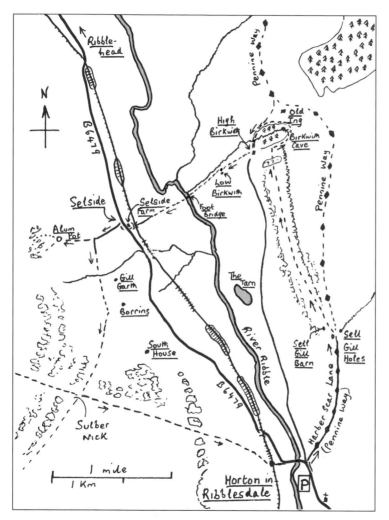

Birkwith Farm, go through the farm gate to join the lane and then, still within the farm area, look for the stile and finger-post on the right signed 'Selside 1¼'. The path goes through a tiny conifer plantation, down to Low Birkwith, through the gate to the right of the farm, into the yard and out again by the gate opposite. This leads to the left bank of the stream, a pleasant ramble alongside it to a footbridge over the Ribble, and then the walled lane up to Selside (signs all the way). Just before reaching the main road, you pass under a railway bridge and immediately beyond it the white-painted building is Selside Farm where you should call to pay your small fee (20p in 1990) to visit Alum Pot. Then turn right up the road and onto the first track on the left.

This tremendous chasm is be found fenced off within the clump of trees beyond, usually with a lively stream pouring into its vertical shaft. On winter days, a cloud of misty spume can make the great pot look like some demonic cauldron. The water from the Alum Pot beck is augmented by that from Long Churn spring pouring into the shaft from an opening about halfway down, and Upper Long Churn Cave can be found by going west from the far (north) side of Alum Pot up the field to a ladder-stile over a wall into a clint field. Cross this leftwards to a few more trees and the spring will be seen entering the cave. The waters flow along this; they originally emerged about 250 yards away in the next field where they submerged again into Lower Long Churn Cave (obviously once all one long cave-passage), but have cut the corner over the years and now only utilise part of the Lower Cave passage before emerging briefly above ground, then vanishing down Diccan Cave, which connects with Alum Pot. It's an interesting overland exploration just to track the flow, but Alum Pot alone is worth 20p of anybody's money any day.

To return, go back towards the road but as soon as you reach the west end of the walled lane used on the approach, turn left (south) down another wall track (grid ref. 779756). The walls soon end and it becomes an open track. When you reach a junction with another track, at a little ford just south of Borrins Farm, make sure you turn right, trending SSW, rising gently across limestone-speckled pastures. Here there are lovely views across Ribblesdale again. When you reach the well-used Sulber Nick path, make a sharp left turn (south-east) and descend over the clints, shelves and grassy pastures which are the last bit of the Three Peaks Walk to Horton in Ribblesdale.

Alum Pot

11.   Pen-y-ghent and Plover Hill

Best map: OS 1:25,000 Yorkshire Dales (Western area)

Distance: 9½ miles/15.2km

Highest elevation reached: 2277ft/694m

Height gained: 1516ft/462m

Overall star rating: **

General level of exertion needed: Medium

Time for the round: About 4½ hours

Terrain: Good path uphill to Pen-y-ghent, rougher with occasional boggier stretches thereafter until the last two miles.

Seen from any direction except the north, Pen-y-ghent is a most shapely and attractive mountain, but to climb up and down it by any of the several paths is, on its own, hardly a full day out, since any reasonably fit person can be on the top in an hour and back in Horton in Ribblesdale inside two with a little effort. Continuing the walk to Plover Hill and then to Foxup Moor – another Pennine watershed with the waters draining one side to the Wharfe and the North Sea, the other side to the Ribble and the Irish Sea – makes for a much more satisfactory walk.

There's a large car park in Horton at the northern end of the village (grid ref. 807726) or, approaching from the south, you may find a spot on a little loop road on the left just before reaching the square-towered and solid-looking church of St Oswald. Wherever you park, take the minor road to the right (east) of the church and on the right side of the beck of Douk Ghyll. (There's no access to this, but from the cave-mouth at its end is a large resurgence of many of the waters draining from the potholes of Pen-y-ghent, including apparently in very wet weather much of that from Hull Pot, which is visited later.) A ten-minute walk up this lane to the farm buildings at Brackenbottom reaches a gate on the left and a sign for Pen-y-ghent. Almost immediately cross a stile, the path goes left and then climbs steadily up pastures beside the wall, over little limestone scarps and then up several sections of wooden walkways built to combat (successfully) the erosion on the boggier ground. As the shoulder of Pen-y-ghent is reached, there's a view of Fountains Fell opposite and then the path climbs up the nab-end of the mountain, first up little ledges at the base of the limestone tier and then over a jumble of gritstone boulders onto the gritstone cap. A final easier trudge leads to the trig point where

From Plover Hill towards Littondale

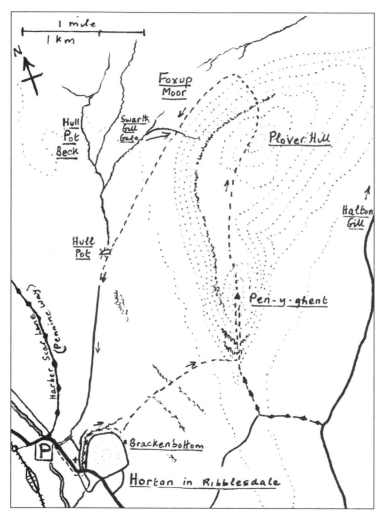

there are fine views, to the west and south in particular.

On the other side of the wall from the trig point, take the footpath signed 'Foxup Rd' which follows the solid gritstone wall, descending northwards and then climbing gently north-eastwards over some fairly slutchy moor, to reach a wall-corner on the highest ground of Plover Hill. There's no cairn although you'll find one if you climb over the wall and continue down the slope to the north-east a little way, and get a grand view down to Halton Gill and Littondale as well.

Now cross a stile in the wall-corner and a few yellow-topped marker-posts continue the northward direction to reach a little gritstone edge, with the sharp outline of Wild Boar Fell on the skyline and views to both Whernside and Ingleborough, the latter with its flat top, before descending steeply to the watershed on Foxup Moor where once again you join a reasonable path.

Going south-west along this soon leads to the stone gatepost at Swarth Gill Gate where waters tumbling from the side of Plover Hill, which have not been swallowed up in the descent, cross the path and shortly join Hull Pot Beck. From the gatepost southwards, follow the path running alongside the wall. This wall fences off Pen-y-ghent Side, undulates over some boggy stretches and then takes a right-angle turn leftwards and heads uphill. The 'Three-Peakers' route, on its way to Whernside, descends to this point from Pen-y-ghent and continues in the same direction

Pen-y-ghent seen from Hull Pot

to cross Hull Pot Beck; so turn sharp right here along it (north-west) and in two minutes reach the beck. A walk downstream along the bank soon leads directly to the huge hole of Hull Pot where, if there's enough water for it not to have been swallowed up in the fissures in the bed of the stream before it reaches the edge of the pot, there is a splendid cascade pouring over the lip in a drop of about sixty feet. This huge rift is about a hundred yards long by twenty wide and the waters, normally disappearing in a sink at the eastern end, have been known actually to fill the great hole to the brim.

Beyond Hull Pot, a green way leads quickly to a gateway and the end of the walled lane used by the Pennine Way. It's an easy and pleasant return along it back to Horton.

12. The Three Peaks Walk

Best map: OS 1:25,000 Yorkshire Dales (Western area)

Distance: About 23 miles/36.8km

Highest elevation reached: 2415ft/736m

Height gained: About 4531ft/1381m

Overall star rating: ***

General level of exertion needed: High to harrowing

Time for the round: 8½–12 hours (see below)

Terrain: A mixture of good tracks, bog, tarmac and bone-jarring clints.

There is a tremendous satisfaction in successfully undertaking a great walk and this book wouldn't have been complete without mentioning it. I have done it five times, my slowest time being nine hours and my best being four hours forty minutes; that day I ran as much as I could and hobbled into Horton in a state of collapse and with muscular cramp. The current record is, I believe, a whisker under two hours thirty minutes.

Unfortunately, the passage of feet since 1887, when the first circuit of the Three Peaks was recorded by two masters from Giggleswick School, has led to increasing erosion of the section over peat moorland. Duckboards and several kinds of experimental protective surfaces have been installed in various places in attempts to contain the damage, although in the long run I feel that only stone slabs – the 'causey-stones' of the old packhorse routes – will be successful. Until this happens, if ever, it is essential that all walkers co-operate in keeping the impact of their own passage to the absolute minimum and, in particular, strictly adhere to sign-posted diversions created to allow the recovery of eroded ground. Given the problems of erosion, I am doubtful whether there should continue to be an annual fell-race over the route. As for mountain bikes (or any bikes), I am now quite certain that they should be banned from this circuit.

As a race, I believe it started at the Hill Inn, Chapel-le-Dale, but as a walk the favourite start has for the last twenty years or so been from the Pen-y-ghent Café in Horton-in-Ribblesdale. This will sound like a plug for the café, and it is since it is justly deserved, for Peter Bayes and his family always have the latest weather forecast available, do smashing hot drinks and food and, at no cost to the walker, operate a clocking-in and clocking-out service.

Let me explain this a bit more: you fill in a registration card which is filed, with your time of departure stamped on it, by an old and now famous

Approaching Pen-y-ghent from Brackenbottom

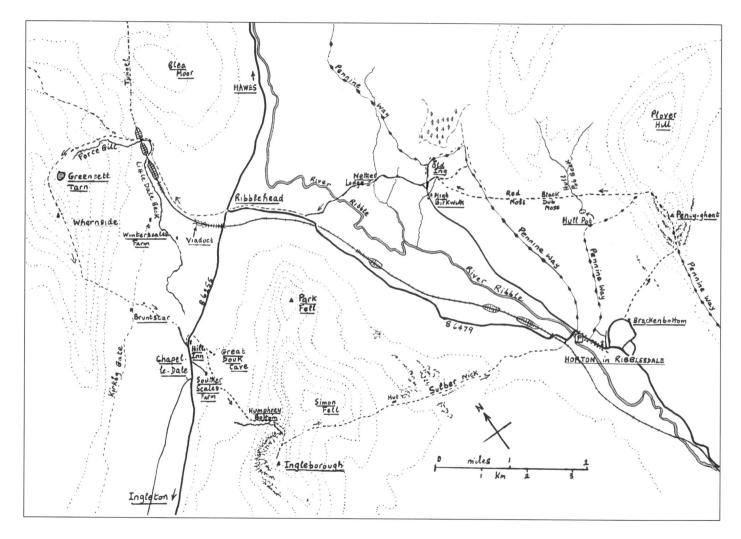

factory clock standing in a corner in the café. The registration card also contains details of your home telephone number (or where you are staying), your car registration number and where you have parked it. If you are an early starter – i.e. before the café is open – you can even pop a written message through the café letter-box; in this case, a card will be made out in your absence, and you will still qualify to join the 'Three Peaks Club' if you return within twelve hours.

The café remains on standby to serve food and drink to walkers 'booked-out'. If any walker – whether you registered personally or in absentia – drops out, say at the Hill Inn, you have *an absolute duty* to either call personally at the café or phone in, because if you fail to do so, you are likely to be presumed to be in trouble. Depending on weather conditions or other relevant circumstances, Peter or his family will look to check if your car has gone or, if you arrived by some other means, will phone the number you left. If they think there is cause for alarm, they notify the police and the Rescue Service may well turn out. The twelve hours' time is a perfectly feasible one for almost everybody but the walk *is* a long one, conditions can change dramatically and it does make sense, particularly if you are a youngster, not very experienced or new to the area, to ensure that someone knows you are out on the hill.

Once the walk has been completed, you can, if you choose, purchase your certificate and badge – but only if you finish inside the twelve hours. A similar arrangement applies to potholing expeditions as well.

The famous clock in the Pen-y-ghent café

I'm happy to say that over the twenty-five years or so that this service has been in operation, little has gone wrong and the police involved only a few times.

What about the route? Well, there are a few places where it has varied over the years and I don't think I've ever gone exactly the same way twice myself but, apart from one major change for the ascent of Whernside, the variations aren't that significant. There are a couple of places, however, where a short but unexpected change of direction can cause you confusion as well so some more detail may be helpful.

Your first hill will be Pen-y-ghent itself (named after the café, of course) so go south down the road from the café or car park (the main one is at grid ref. 807726 at the north end of the village) and then, as described in Walk 11, head for the church and then left up the lane to Brackenbottom. The path is signed from here, a steady climb up the scars (and nowadays over the duckboards on stilts (how I wish they were flat limestone blocks instead) with a final roughish scramble to the top of the hill. In about 2½ miles/4.3km you'll gain about 1516ft/462m.

The next section is the crunch and one of the reasons that I think Horton is the best starting-place for the walk is so this section is done early in the day.

Pen-y-ghent to Whernside summit (the roof of Yorkshire) is almost 11 miles/17.6km and for almost 7 miles/11.2km you are either descending or are more or less on the level. From the trig point on Pen-y-ghent, head north along the west edge of the fell and in half a mile you'll see the Pennine Way path on the slopes below but also a less-used path trending further right (to the north-west) and running fairly close to a wall. Take this one; it crosses the Swarth Gill Gate to Horton path (see Walk 11), crosses Hull Pot Beck and, keeping in the same direction over Black Dub Moss and Red Moss, quits the bogs, reaches the limestone and the Pennine Way track at grid ref. 811762. This is one of the places where confusion can occur and there is a kink in the route whichever way you choose. Less usually, you may turn north and follow the Pennine Way for just over half a mile before turning left (west) to Old Ing Farm. Here you must leave the Pennine Way, go slightly downhill towards High Birkwith Farm and take the good track on the right (i.e. turning back north-west) and heading now for Nether Lodge. Or, more directly, cross the Pennine Way, still going north-west and you will join the track that runs round the head of Birkwith Gill (see also Walk 10) just below Old Ing. Turn downhill now towards High Birkwith at the foot of the gill but regain the north-west direction by turning right again at the good track reached just before entering the farmyard and heading for Nether Lodge.

The track crosses the natural arch of God's Bridge over the Brow Gill Beck, continues to Nether Lodge Farm and then the track leads over the River Ribble to the attractive old house of Ingman Lodge, just beyond which is a spring and a trough of welcome drinking water. You reach the road almost immediately at grid ref. 777782. I personally hate the

Whernside and the Ribblehead Viaduct in winter

tarmac bit that follows and if the proposed route from Nether Lodge to Thorns, Ribblehead House and then over the lower part of Blea Moor ever becomes reality it will be an improvement, I think. In the meantime, it's just over a mile/1.6km on the road, needing care because of traffic, to the mighty Batty Moss (Ribblehead) Viaduct.

The next section – and the way I always used to go – took a very direct line to the north-west along the rough track underneath the viaduct to Gunnerfleet Farm, then almost to Winterscales Farm, turned south-west just before reaching it and then turned right (north-west) again to go straight up the moor.

This part of the route was on a permissive path, not a right of way, and over the years it became unbelievably eroded, an awful black and oozing scar on the landscape. The permission to use it has therefore been withdrawn to allow it to recover, so don't plan to take that route.

The path to take nowadays doesn't go under the viaduct but stays alongside the railway to cross it by the aqueduct carrying the waters of Force Gill to Little Dale Beck. It follows the old track of the Craven Way for half a mile and then curves off to the west, climbing steadily and swinging south to reach the main ridge of Whernside just above Greensett

Tarn. The going is mostly much firmer than the old direct route and the scenery is much more attractive so it's no hardship to have to add a little in distance. By the time you've reached the top you will have about 13½ miles/21.6km under your feet and 3110ft/948m of altitude.

It's about 5 miles/8km and 1421ft/433m to Ingleborough's summit now and the descent from Whernside hasn't changed from the one I've always used; it's just improved: a steep and obvious path leading down the ridge to the south and then directly to Bruntscar Farm, crossing the track of the Kirkby Gate, down to Philpin Lane and a junction with the Hawes road. Your tongue will be hanging out and you won't need telling that the Hill Inn is just up the road to the left.

From the inn, continue north-east towards Ribblehead, turn off right in 200 yards or so at the sign for Great Douk Cave and head directly south towards the shapely Ingleborough, seen ahead. The path leads over delightful limestone clints and pasture, keeping right of an obvious wall coming down from Simon Fell and then, over boggier ground, climbs steeply up a loose and scruffy gully from Humphrey Bottom onto the lower part of the summit plateau (see also Walk 5). The stretch from Pen-y-ghent to Whernside may have been the psychological crux but this steep pull up Ingleborough is a b— at the end of the day. Fortunately the top is now near at hand, reached by swinging south-west up the last bit of the ridge. Just before reaching the plateau, take note where the descent path heads off the ridge to the east, then you can climb the last little bit and walk happily over to touch the summit trig point.

Sounds straightforward enough, doesn't it? So it is when the weather is clear. It can be very different, however, if the weather is unfavourable and I don't want anybody to think that it's always just a doddle. I once climbed Ingleborough from the Hill Inn and, because there was a lot of snow on the ground, I followed that solid wall up to the plateau edge, the one nearer to Simon Fell than the way I've just described. The mist and a high wind developed, I became confused and, to cut a long story short, I finished up in Selside on the wrong side of the mountain. It was a long walk back along the road and I learnt the vital lesson of taking compass bearings *before* losing visibility, not after.

All that remains is the 4½ miles/7.2km or so back to Horton, so retrace your steps from the summit north-eastwards and find the path that slants across the soggy moorland slope of Simon Fell. Bog and peat give way to limestone clints after about a mile and a half, near a derelict wooden shooting-hut, then you shortly pass through the cutting or depression in the limestone of Sulber Nick. It's much harder on your aching feet now but it's not long before you cross a last limestone shelf and are on an undulating path across grassy pastures, leading to a surprise finish crossing of the railway line at Horton Station. The mugs of tea and big butties await and in a day or two, as the pain wears off, you'll feel great. Just writing about it now makes me realise that I'll just have to do it again.

Ingleborough from near the Hill Inn

13.   Smearsett, Pot and Giggleswick Scars

Best map: OS 1:25,000 Yorkshire Dales (Western area)

Distance: About 8 miles/12.8km

Highest elevation reached: 1191ft/363m

Height gained: 528ft/161m

Overall star rating: * *

General level of exertion needed: Medium/easy

Time for the round: About 4 hours

Terrain: Mostly good paths on grass; many stiles.

This very good walk links three fine natural limestone escarpments and the 'Celtic Wall' – of great antiquity and in an isolated setting – with a return along the lovely valley of the River Ribble.

Start at Stainforth (car park at grid ref. 821673) on the B6479 Settle to Horton in Ribblesdale road. Walk north up the main road, then take the first turn left (west) along a lane which crosses the Settle–Carlisle railway and allows a brief view of the conical top of Smearsett Scar to the north-west; this is an old packhorse way from Ribblesdale to Feizor and Austwick. It crosses the River Ribble by the elegant Stainforth Bridge and though the waterfall is only just downstream it will be better seen on the return.

Continue past the caravan site and Knight Stainforth Hall and keep straight ahead up the rough walled lane signed for Feizor. This leads to open pasture up which a green track climbs towards the north-west. Climb the stile at the top of the rise and then an isolated, short but solid length of wall can be clearly seen, half-left on the skyline ahead. From a distance it is just an oddity, but make your way over to it; closer acquaintance shows it to be of great age, its limestone blocks much worn by the elements. The remains of possibly Celtic (pre-Roman) earthworks have apparently been discovered below nearby Pot Scar, so the Celtic Wall may either be part of an ancient defensive system (there is another wall fragment nearby) or possibly have something to do with ancient burial practices. The route now goes to Smearsett Scar via a ladder-stile in a wall-corner and a scramble leads up to the trig point; its modest summit has a fine viewpoint.

The limestone edges now lead on, curving and with a dip in the middle, to the top of Pot Scar; the village of Feizor is seen sheltering below. The way now slopes towards thick woods ahead with steep crags on the left (Pot Scar is a haunt of rock-climbers) and reaches a scooped-out valley where the edge curves round and

Along Giggleswick Scar from Buck Haw Brow

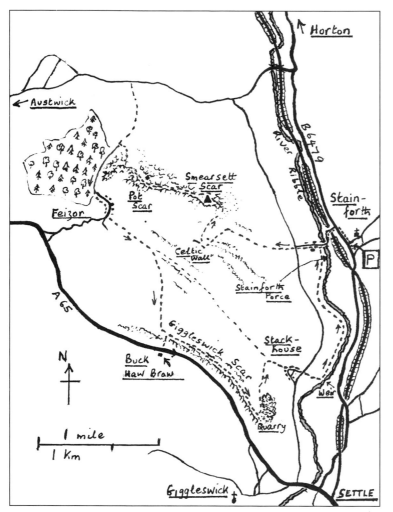

meets a substantial wall. A direct descent to Feizor from here would be straightforward but a stile over the wall into the lane has been diverted into somebody's back garden. So don't descend but instead take the gap-stile through the wall ahead and bear right (north) down a rocky field to a gate in its corner and so reach the lane leading north–south through the gap of Feizor Nick. Turn left (south) here into the pretty village and take the signed path for Stackhouse, just beyond Scar Close Farm.

A green way now climbs gently away from Feizor and continues directly to Stackhouse, but when you reach it, follow the signed bridleway bearing right (south). This leads across fields with gates until the land drops away ahead; here you reach the A65 (the old main road not the new by-pass) at Buck Haw Brow, and Giggleswick Scar stretches away to the east above the road.

Turn east now, following the scar along a broad shelf, passing Kinsey Cave's wide entrance seen up a side valley, two smaller caves and the vertical fissure of Wall Cave until, just before reaching the large cairn of Schoolboys Tower, the tremendous quarry workings loom just ahead. Follow marker-posts to avoid them, but then bear left on a track which swings north-east and then north, with Pen-y-ghent now in view. Take a line towards the village of Stackhouse, just below the highest land and just above some woods. This track soon becomes a path, passes a large dew-pond made of cracked concrete, continues just outside the wood and then, as it fades

Smearsett Scar seen from the Celtic Wall

away into the pasture, use either a stile or the gate just beyond it and descend steeply sloping fields to Stackhouse.

Here a stony track between high walls and elegant houses leads to a minor T-junction where a left and immediate right turn quickly leads down a walled lane to the locks and a weir over the Ribble. Take the path over the stone stile, and the four more which follow, along the left bank of the river; this leads to a lovely green sward beneath beech trees, with Langcliffe Mill on the other bank. This is now a paper-mill but it was the subject of an inter-monastic row some centuries ago which was so bitter that appeal had to be made to the Pope to settle it.

Finally, after one short detour away from the river bank, keep outside the wall near the caravan park where the river emerges from a gorge. Just beyond are the cascades of Stainforth Force and the elegant Stainforth Bridge. The car park is soon reached, and the end of a delightful walk.

14. Fountains Fell and Malham Tarn

Best map: OS 1:25,000 Yorkshire Dales (Southern area)

Distance: About 8½ miles/13.6km

Highest elevation reached: 2192ft/668m

Height gained: 1276ft/389m

Overall star rating: */**

General level of exertion needed: Medium/high

Time for the round: About 4½ hours.

Terrain: A mixture of sometimes boggy paths on the gritstone moorland and good ones on the limestone.

This walk contrasts fine limestone scenery near Malham Tarn with that on the high grit-capped moorland of Fountains Fell. This latter is especially interesting and I certainly do not want to miss it out but it is not possible at present to construct a good 'round' over it without involving either an unacceptable amount of tarmac bashing or too great a distance. So this walk is shaped more like a fish-hook and – unless you've got a 'chauffeur' – transport needs to be arranged. Parties could start at each end and swap keys midway, or leave one car at one end and all travel in the second to the start. Perhaps the best plan, and the way the walk is described, is to be dropped off near Darnbrook House (grid ref. 899705) or you could park just off the roadside up the hill beyond, towards Arncliffe. Your eventual pick-up will be on the Stainforth to Halton Gill road, where the Pennine Way crosses it and there is plenty of roadside parking (grid ref. 842715).

Leave the road where it starts to climb the hill (south-west) beyond Darnbrook House and find the path on the left, shadowing Darnbrook Beck. This crosses the Cowside Beck by a footbridge and climbs quite steeply for a short way up the side of the gill, breaking through a fringe of limestone scars and then more gently over grassy limestone pasture to join the Monk's Road (see Walk 39). This now leads to where the buildings of Middle House shelter in a clump of trees. Follow the track round left and down the slope beyond; you get a glimpse of Malham Tarn, the next objective, to the right of Great Close Hill. A gate and stile lead down towards Middle House Farm and opposite this is a three-way finger-post at a fence and stile and this indicates 'FP Malham Tarn ¾' to the south-west. The Monk's Road path continues from here; it's faint but shadows the telephone-wire posts over a low saddle, to reach the Pennine Way path at

Pen-y-ghent from the top of Fountains Fell

73

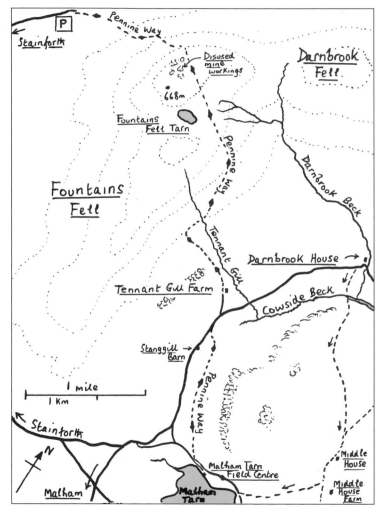

the side of Malham Tarn, just as it passes into the woods of Malham Tarn House (Field Studies Centre). Follow the track beyond the buildings until a Pennine Way sign points through a gate on the right, just before the buildings at Water Houses. A path now leads pleasantly across fields below the scars of West End, passes Stangill Barn and reaches the road just before Tennant Gill.

Ahead now, beyond a few remaining bright green fields and a line of white limestone scars, lies a darker landscape. The Pennine Way path leads past the farm and up the field, goes sharply left after a gate and then upwards to the north-east across sheep pasture. It then swings north and slants gently towards the shoulder of the fell, the ground becoming much peatier and wetter as the gritstone layers are reached. A prominent cairn on a hillock marks a change of direction to the north-west and shortly afterwards two stone men, rather like a pair of gateposts, come into sight on the highest land ahead. On the plateau to the south of here, and hidden unless you go searching for it, is Fountains Fell Tarn. But the extraordinary landscape just ahead is not hidden. Despite the healing effects of time, the land to the south-west still looks like a First World War battlefield, with endless humps and craters amidst typical Pennine groughs and peat hags.

It is almost impossible to imagine coal-mining without machines and motor vehicles but right on the top of this wild, bleak moor, over 2000ft above sea level, miners walked four and five miles up the moor to start a day's work and back again at night, and the coal was transported on horseback down the hill. It was mined from bell-pits and although most of the narrow shafts have collapsed into the 'bell' at the bottom of the pit, thus forming the craters all round, two of them are fenced off and quite visible. The coal would have been used for the calcining of lime in the kilns which are to be found all over the limestone country of the Dales, and date from the time of the agricultural revolution of the eighteenth century. Nearby is the solid stone-built coke-oven, erected nearly two hundred years ago to provide coke for the processing of the zinc ore being mined on Pikedaw Hill above Malham.

A huge cairn at 2192ft/668m marks the highest point on this vast plateau and is reached by either plodding round the peat hags or slithering both up and down them. But once you have found your way to the edge, where the land drops very steeply, the view of Pen-y-ghent is the finest of all; you can enjoy this view while negotiating the slanting descent path to the west, down to the road where you hope your transport awaits.

*Looking north-west from
Fountains Fell*

Cautley Crag from Yarlside

PART TWO

The Howgills, Baugh Fell and Mallerstang

15. Yarlside and the Eastern Howgills

Best map: 1:40,000 Harvey Mountain Map
(Howgill Fells) which covers the whole walk.
Alternatives are OS 1:25,000 Pathfinders 617
(Sedbergh and Baugh Fell) sheet SD 69/79
plus 607 (Tebay and Kirkby Stephen) sheet
NY 60/70; both are needed. Or OS 1:50,000
Landrangers 91 (Appleby-in-Westmorland)
and 98 (Wensleydale and Upper Wharfedale)

Distance: About 8 miles/12.8km

Highest elevation reached: 2096ft/639m

Height gained: 1680ft/512m

Overall star rating: ★★★

General level of exertion needed: Medium/high

Time for the round: About 4½ hours

Terrain: About half the walk is on fair paths and
tracks; the rest is on the open, grassy fell.
Avoid in misty weather.

This is a superb round, with marvellous scenery
and views and, in clear weather, should give no
route-finding problems once the descent from Yarlside
to Kensgriff is over.

Park near the Cross Keys Inn (grid ref. 698969)
about 4 miles towards Kirkby Stephen from Sedbergh
on the A683, at the end of the valley containing the
cirque of Cautley Crag and Spout. Cross the footbridge over the River Rawthey as though heading for
the Spout but immediately leave the footpath and
tackle the grassy slope of Ben End which rises directly
ahead and forms the right arm of the cirque. The
initial angle is steep but it is straightforward going on
the short grass which is typical of the Howgills; the
ascent soon eases, allowing grand views of the Crag
and Spout.

From the little heap of stones on Ben End, a short
descent and then a pull up the other slope leads to the
more substantial cairn on the fine summit of Yarlside.
And what a view! Across the grain of the country and
all the transverse valleys and fells to the west: to Wild
Boar Fell, Swarth Fell and Baugh Fell to the east;
along the deep valley of Bowderdale to the north.
Take care here, though, for the easy slope of the ridge
to the north-west, which seems the straightforward
continuation of the walk, leads downhill too far into
Bowderdale. Instead, you must swing sharply north
(and the path may not be obvious) to make a steep
descent to the Saddle, which separates Yarlside from
the little peak of Kensgriff. Beyond the ascent to
Kensgriff, a further downhill slope leads to another

*Gills on the flank of
Wandale Hill seen from
Kensgriff*

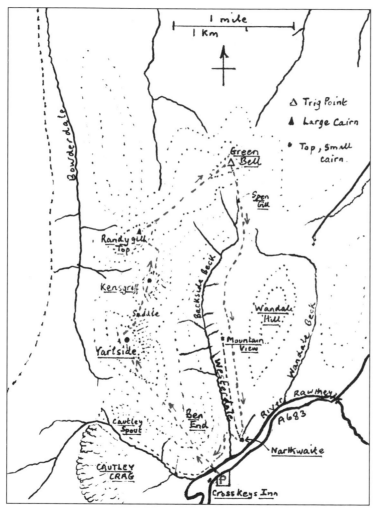

hause and then an obvious climb to the large cairn on rounded Randygill Top.

I followed a fox's tracks in the snow here once. Perhaps he was doing this round too, for he'd been to the stones on Randygill Top and then on the almost level path on the ridge out to the white-painted trig point on Green Bell. Here he'd stood and looked out over the fields of the Stainmore Gap, as I did, to the northern Pennines beyond. Then he'd chosen the best line back to the south, down the incipient Spen Gill to a lower hause where there's a wall (unusual on these fells) at the head of Adamthwaite Sike. At one point I thought he'd taken a different path but the spoor reappeared alongside the wet and rushy track on the west side of Wandale Hill; this track quickly improves and leads easily to the uninhabited, sadly dilapidated and well-named farmstead of Mountain View. Here I could no longer see his tracks and my dogs Henry and Freddie soon forgot the fox too as they started to look for rabbits instead.

The economics of hill-farming are precarious at the best of times and the ruins of farms like this are to be found on the higher marginal land in Mallerstang, Grisedale and many other places in the Dales. The trend seems set to continue and with it the decline of a way of life which has shaped the landscape for centuries. We may yet see stretches of the higher land reverting to natural woodland and forest, their saplings not eaten by sheep any more; I fear, however, that the woods are more likely to be of dreary conifers.

Don't go through either of the two gates leading to

'Mountain View' and the slopes of Yarlside

Mountain View but stay outside the intake wall, following sheep tracks alongside it and going steadily down the flank of Westerdale. When the wall turns downhill, a grassy terrace continues the best line; when a fork is reached, the right-hand side leads to a gate, the wall again and a good path leading to a last section of walled lane into the farmyard at Narthwaite. Go immediately out of the yard by turning back sharp right and downhill to a gate, a little waterfall and beside it a ford across the Backside Beck. Be prepared for a quick dash across the stream here if the water level is high, for there aren't any stepping-stones and that's the only chance you'll have of not ending up with sodden feet. But it's only a short distance now back to the Cross Keys; once over the water, swing back downstream again on the path on the opposite bank and it leads round the lowest slopes of Ben End and back to the start.

16.   Cautley Spout and The Calf

Best maps: OS 1:25,000 Pathfinder 617 (Sedbergh and Baugh Fell) sheet SD 69/79. Also on 1:40,000 Harvey Mountain Map (Howgill Fells); and OS 1:50,000 Landranger 98 (Wensleydale & Upper Wharfedale)

Distance: About 5½ miles/8.8km

Highest elevation reached: 2218ft/676m

Height gained: 1637ft/499m

Overall star rating: * * *

General level of exertion needed: Medium/high

Time for the round: About 3½–4 hours

Terrain: Good paths most of the way, otherwise grassy slopes. Great care is needed in misty weather since navigation is notoriously tricky on these hills.

Cautley Spout is one of the longest waterfalls in England, although it is made up of a succession of cascades pouring through a breach in the mile-long cliff of Cautley Crag. This is made up of a series of broken and vegetated crumbling rock buttresses sweeping round in a shallow cirque and is the largest mass of exposed rock in these generally grass-covered hills. The crags are of little interest to a rock-climber but are easily the most impressive sight available in the Howgills to the passing traveller. A walker with a bit of energy visiting the falls is also within a comparatively short distance of the highest point of the massif, The Calf, and can consequently make a splendid round suitable for a short day.

The car-parking area is at the roadside near to the excellent and friendly Cross Keys Inn about four miles out of Sedbergh on the A683 to Kirkby Stephen (grid ref. 698969) and the hollow sweep of Cautley Crag, with the thin ribbon of the Spout partly visible, immediately commands attention, even before you've got your boots on. Walk north up the road for a few yards to the footbridge over the River Rawthey and swing left along a normally wet track which leads round the lowest slopes of Ben End and then up the right bank of Cautley Holme Beck. There is almost no gain in height until you have penetrated quite a way into the combe, then tongues of grassy scree rise steeply ahead.

You can now either cross the stream and scramble very steeply up the left (west) side for a really good view of the falls. However, there is no real path this way; the route is taken only by masochistic photo-enthusiasts since the view of the falls from the other

Towards Bowderdale from above Cautley Crag

83

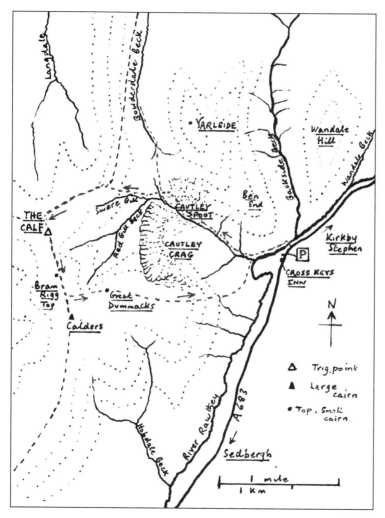

side is more masked by vegetation. Or, more easily, follow the steep path winding up the right-hand side; this still allows good views, including the 90-ft leap of the longest fall. An even more sedate approach may be made by following a track up further right to Bowderdale Head and then contouring back to the top of the falls.

Two gills, Red Gill and Swere Gill, meet just before the breach through the crags and paths now follow them both. If the weather is clear and the broad dome of The Calf is the next objective, keep going (west) up the right-hand of the two, Swere Gill, then when it bends left head straight up the slope to connect with an obvious slanting path usually visible, at least in clear weather, from below. This is the line of an old track from Bowderdale over the Howgills and, once reached, it leads across the highest plateau, passing a little tarn en route and, just as the Romans couldn't be bothered with peak-bagging but always took the direct military line, it bypasses the summit of The Calf. However, modern walkers want to reach the top so there is now an obvious path. It's worth a visit for a splendid if distant view of Lakeland.

A well-worn path, the 'motorway' route to The Calf from Sedbergh, is now used going south to Bram Rigg Top and then, where the latter continues south to the large cairn on Calders, use the fence-line going east out to the fourth summit of Great Dummacks. The slopes from this drop away rather steeply to end in a plunge over Cautley Crag so it is advisable to swing a little south on leaving the top, after which steep grassy slopes overlooking the cirque lead down to a good track contouring the fellside and an easy return to the Cross Keys.

As an illustration of the possible navigational problems, I came here once on a misty day with my wife and a friend. I went up the left side of the Spout and continued up that side to the top of the falls. The others went up the right side and, tired of waiting for me and my camera, they continued up Red Gill Beck to Great Dummacks and then descended as described above. I thought they'd gone to The Calf, couldn't even find that in the mist, so returned on a prayer and compass bearing to Cautley Spout. I contoured round the rim of the Crag, looking for them in vain, before descending. I found them, tucking into tea and scones in the Cross Keys. 'What kept you?' they asked.

Cautley Spout

17. Baugh Fell: The Waterfalls Walk

Best maps: 1:40,000 Harvey Mountain Map
   (Howgill Fells) or OS 1:25,000 Pathfinder 617
   (Sedbergh and Baugh Fell) sheet SD 69/79.
   Also on 1:50,000 Landranger 98
   (Wensleydale & Upper Wharfedale)

Distance: About 11 miles/17.6km

Highest elevation reached: 2218ft/676m

Height gained: 1526ft/465m

Overall star rating: **

General level of exertion needed: Medium/high

Time for the round: About six hours

Terrain: Mostly over rough grassy moorland with
   few paths.

To look at the sprawling, apparently featureless mass of Baugh Fell from a distance or on the map one could be forgiven for thinking it should be spelt 'Bore Fell'. There may be no fine crags or edges, it is true, but to track the River Rawthey to its source almost at the top of the fell is to visit (apart from other delights) no fewer than nine waterfalls on the ascent alone, and the best (which is very fine and certainly far better than many famous Dales falls) isn't even named on the map. I once did this walk in the rain and heavy mist and, for five hours, was unable to see more than thirty yards ahead but I still found it to be a walk of absorbing interest. Given clear visibility, it certainly deserves greater attention than it receives at present.

Start from just west of Rawthey Bridge on the Sedbergh to Kirkby Stephen road (A683) where there is a large space at the side of the road (grid ref. 714979). Just across the road is a sign for 'Uldale and Bluecaster Side' pointing not up the River Rawthey but to the south-west. This is the way to start: it is the old road leading towards Sedbergh known as 'The Street'. Then, after just a short distance, swing left (ESE) towards the river on a faint tractor track. This leads in the direction needed at a higher level across the moor and then slowly descends towards the river, reaching it at a wooden bridge across a little gorge and a series of attractive small cascades just upstream.

The next mile or so is particularly attractive. Stay with the sketchy path on the west bank, shortly passing a 20-ft waterfall and then the ruined buildings of a tiny quarry. The waters of Whin Stone Gill next join the main flow by way of a fine little waterfall on the far bank and, further ahead where the stream now flows in a more steeply-sided ravine, can be seen more

Baugh Fell seen from Rise Hill

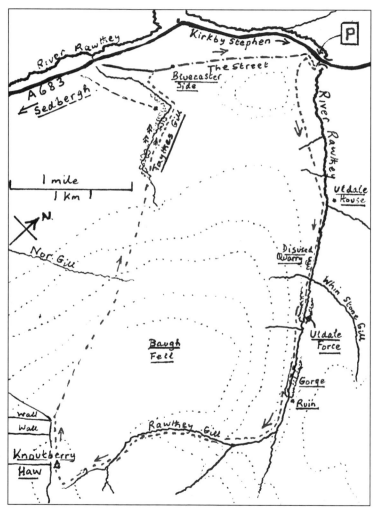

cascades. The path now becomes very narrow and leads towards them across steep grass slopes and into a superb semi-circular rock amphitheatre fringed with little limestone scars. Here the waters of the Rawthey spill over a sharp lip in the splendid 30-ft waterfall of Uldale Force (grid ref. 736958) – a fine sight at any time.

To escape from the amphitheatre will require a steep scramble over the limestone edge fringing it, and more nervous walkers will retreat a little to find easier ground as a means of gaining the higher land above the falls, where a bit of a path will be found leading on again. More open views are now ahead and a fine, long limestone gorge is soon reached. Little cliffs crowd into this at several points, making walking up it an exciting expedition because of the need to boulder-hop from one side of the stream to the other. Quite suddenly, the gorge ends with an old ruin up on the left bank and the high land of Swarth Fell looming above it.

For half a mile now the river is just an ordinary moorland stream until it takes a sharp turn to the right (south-west) and then it can be seen coming down another long steep-sided ravine, marked on the OS 1:50,000 map as Rawthey Gill. It's best to stay close to the water's edge and generally on the west bank, passing two more short but fine cascades on the way. Although it is a further two miles to the end of the longest dwindling trickle, it never becomes boring and you are not aware of the vast desolation of the fell-top until you are completing the gentle climb to the wall seen ahead. Turn right (south-west) along-side the wall and the trig point on Knoutberry Haw, the highest point, will soon (thank heavens) be reached.

Having had, I hope, clear weather and so have seen the views, continue north-west alongside the wall, but (at grid ref. 726922) when this turns down Ring-ing Keld Gutter to the west, the featureless nature of the great Baugh Fell becomes very apparent: miles of cotton-grass and not much else, no walls, but no obstacles either. I once walked from here in thick mist on a compass bearing (about north-west) for two and a half miles and reached the head of Taythes Gill bang on target.

Hopefully you'll have a fine day and a clear view of the way across the long, long, sloping fellside towards the green of Taythes Beck Wood. Taythes Gill is delightful and has yet another fine waterfall. Once you've crossed to the sheep track on the eastern bank, above the trees and away from the farm, a little path wanders down the valley until it seems to end in a grassy hollow. Climb up out of this; just over the top is The Street again. A right turn along here, past the farm at Bluecaster Side, and it is an almost level walk along the old track back to the car.

Uldale Force, Baugh Fell

18. Round of the Western Howgills

Best maps: OS 1:25,000 Pathfinder 617 (Sedbergh and Baugh Fell) sheet SD 69/79. Also on 1:40,000 Harvey Mountain Map (Howgill Fells) and OS 1:50,000 Landrangers 97 (Kendal to Morecambe) plus 98 (Wensleydale & Upper Wharfedale); both are needed

Distance: About 9.3 miles/15km (or 8 miles/12.8km for the shorter round)

Highest elevation reached: 2218ft/676m

Height gained: 1578ft/481m

Overall star rating: * *

General level of exertion needed: Medium

Time for the round: About 5 hours (or 4½ hours for the shorter round)

Terrain: Almost all on grass or grassy paths. Avoid misty weather; this is a round which is obvious when clear but can be a nightmare in mist.

The geography of the western Howgills is fairly complex, but south of Carlin Gill (the old county boundary and the line also adopted as the boundary of the Yorkshire Dales National Park) they are all drained by Chapel Beck and its tributaries. The crest above these gives a fine complete round starting and finishing at the same place, with no tarmac bashing, and takes in the six tops of Arant Haw, Calders, Bram Rigg Top, The Calf, White Fell Head and Fell Head. It is certainly an outstanding skyline round for the discerning walker on a clear day. Howgill Lane is too narrow for a coach and there is only parking room for a few cars.

The start is at Birkhaw Farm (grid ref. 638947) just off Howgill Lane, the narrow Roman road that skirts the foot of the Howgill Fells from Sedbergh going north to Tebay. Howgill Lane is too narrow for more than a few cars to park but you may park up in the farmyard; ask nicely and offer to pay, for the farmer and his wife are very helpful and prefer you to do this rather than obstruct the lane lower down. A track now leads through a gate beyond the farm and its trees, alongside a little beck, through two more gates in quick succession and then bears left, heading north-east alongside a wall to a little ford (next to a sheepfold), beyond which is the open fell.

The track forks just past the ford and this is a moment of decision. The main track goes left (north), taking a lower line below the little hill of Seat Knott, descends slightly to another ford and sheepfold and then climbs up onto the broad grassy

The western Howgills skyline seen from Seat Knott

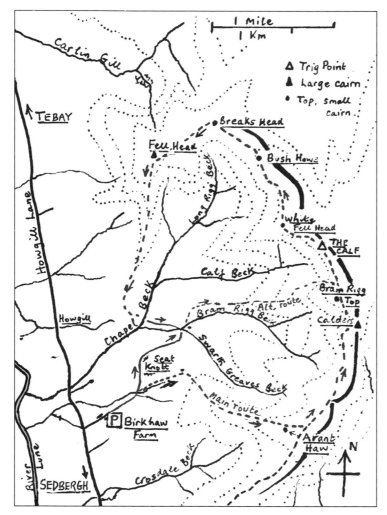

ridge of Bram Rigg, leading north-east to Bram Rigg Top. To go this way gives a shorter round and misses out two good tops (Arant Haw and Calders), but there is a track and if you need the comfort of that, then that is the way for you: it's still a splendid round.

For the full round, take the right-hand uphill track just past the ford and climb (north-east) to the little col (with a corrugated-iron sheepfold) between Seat Knott and a long ridge descending from Arant Haw which is south-east of this point. Now climb this ridge which overlooks Swarth Greaves Beck and has a fine view to all the traffic revving along the M6 only about three miles away across the River Lune, to a high point which isn't the top but is a good place to sit and rest for a minute while you literally watch the world rush past below. Then with just a little more effort you reach Arant Haw and the main ridge. Just over the top is a broad track which descends to a col, then climbs alongside a stout wire fence (this encloses the head of Hobdale and is the only fence or wall anywhere on these fells) up to the large cairn on Calders. Leaving the fence, now head just east of north, on a path across broad grassy moor, on to Bram Rigg Top. A short descent to a col then a little climb on an obvious path leads up to The Calf and the trig point. It's the highest point of the Howgills and, for long-range views in particular, an outstanding situation on a clear day: the Lakeland peaks around Scafell Pike, which are about thirty miles away, can be picked out on the northern arc, while the Three Peaks are about fifteen miles away on the southern.

On the descent from Fell Head looking back towards The Calf

Much of this fine prospect remains in view as you head north-west now along the main spine (crossing the old Bowderdale–Chapel Beck path) first to White Fell Head, then high above all the little gills draining into Long Rigg Beck (which becomes Chapel Beck lower down), over Bush Howe and up to Breaks Head (grid ref. 654985, and not named on OS 1:50,000). Here the path takes a sharp turn left (south-west) towards a large and obvious cairn on Fell Head. To the north, the view is down towards the dramatic gorge of Carlin Gill; to the south, you may look back across most of the great cirque that you have traversed during the walk.

From Fell Head take a long grassy ridge (the retaining wall of Long Rigg Gill), where there is no path but is easy going; it leads to the SSW, with a steeper bit at the bottom, down to Chapel Beck at the point where the track seen descending the facing slope of White Fell crosses the stream. Cross the stream here, but then curve round eastwards on a path and track to the sheepfold at the foot of Bram Rigg Beck, to join the main track back to Birkhaw Farm.

19. Carlin Gill and Black Force

Best maps: 1:40,000 Harvey Mountain Map (Howgill Fells). Alternatively, OS 1:25,000 Pathfinders 617 (Sedbergh and Baugh Fell) sheet SD 69/79 plus 607 (Tebay and Kirkby Stephen) sheet NY 60/70; both are needed. Or OS 1:50,000 Landrangers 97 (Kendal to Morecambe) plus 91 (Appleby-in-Westmorland) plus 98 (Wensleydale & Upper Wharfedale); all three are needed – which is why the Harvey map is such a bonus

Distance: About 7½ miles/12km

Highest elevation reached: 2044ft/623m (or, as given on the Harvey map 2106ft/642m)

Height gained: 1470ft/448m

Overall star rating: * * *

General level of exertion needed: Medium/high

Time for the round: About 4½ hours

Terrain: Fair path up Carlin Gill, then rough scrambling at its head. Largely pathless but easy walking on grass thereafter. Avoid in misty weather.

The head of Carlin Gill is superbly dramatic mountain country. The gill itself is incut deeply into the soft, rolling Howgill Fells, has its own fine cascade, The Spout, at its head and would make an interesting enough walk on its own. But the addition of the splendid gill and waterfall of Black Force, where the Little Ulgill Beck pours down a dramatic gash in the northern flank of Fell Head into the upper part of Carlin Gill, turns this walk into an exciting expedition.

Park just south of the cattle-grid where the road makes a sharp kink at the end of Carlin Gill (grid ref. 625995), most easily reached from the north along Howgill Lane, off the A685 Tebay–Kendal road.

The first hundred yards up the gill from the bridge may be awkward if there's much water in it so cut round the north slope of Gibbet Hill (where only a few centuries ago sheep-stealers and other criminals were hanged and their corpses dangled in chains) and slope into the bed of the gill a little higher up. Then a path stays very close to the stream, switching from one side to the other for, although the gill bed is pretty level for some time, the gill sides are very steep.

After about a mile, a fork is reached and a series of cascades from Small Gill on the right join Carlin Gill, which here bends to the left. Now the ravine becomes even steeper, its bed almost choked with trees, and

Looking down Little Ulgill Beck from Fell Head

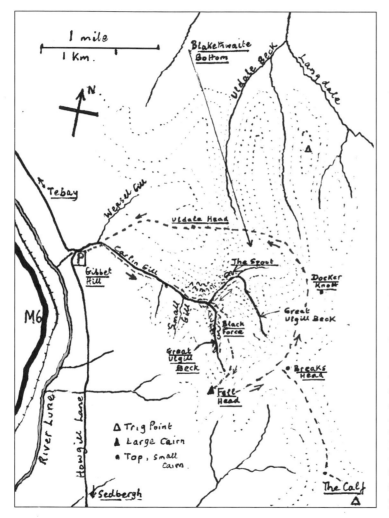

rising beyond these is what looks like a deep combe, having a long, shattered rock buttress slanting from bottom left to top right and topped by grass. Keep close to the stream and you will be able to scramble quite easily along its rocky bed until, emerging from the trees, it will be seen that the slanting rock buttress is in fact the left side of another tremendous ravine, that of Black Force. Facing north, the sun rarely penetrates here and the bare black rocks glint with spray as the waters at the head of the gill pour through a portal formed by two smooth but contorted rock buttresses and then tumble down a series of rocky ledges and boulders.

Improbable as it may seem there are two escape routes up here, but before contemplating either continue a little further up the main gill on a sketchy path. Round a bend a fine sight is revealed: the waters of Little Ulgill Beck shoot over a rock lip in another waterfall about forty feet high. This is called, accurately but prosaically, The Spout, and it is certainly worth the little extra effort needed to have a look.

Return now to the foot of Black Force. On a warm summer day the actual bed of the gill gives a fine scramble, going up the right-hand side of the watercourse and crossing over to the left just above the main waterfall, then directly upwards, with some harder moves near the top. The walking route, however, takes a sketchy path winding up the grassy spur on the left of the cascades (the top of the buttress seen from lower down). This is steep but easy, narrowing into a little arete at the top, and has spectacular views down the gill and across to the great slabs of rock whose contortions are now seen to be the result of colossal folding forces on the earth's crust.

Follow the gill now as it winds much more gently into a wide grassy bowl, using a bit of a path for some of the way, then climb pathless slopes to Fell Head, the highest point of this part of the Howgills, where there's a large cairn and a marvellous view all round the great cirque of fells, including The Calf, all of which are drained by Chapel Beck to the River Lune.

A path leaves Fell Head which goes north-east at first and you should follow it for ten minutes or so to Breaks Head (grid ref. 654985, and not named on OS 1:50,000 map), where it turns right (south-east) along the main ridge towards The Calf. Leave this path here and go instead in a northerly direction on the high land which bounds Great Ulgill Beck on its east flank. This leads easily and naturally in a gentle curving line towards the round top of Docker Knott but descend before reaching it to the broad flat and grassy hause of Blakethwaite Bottom; this is drained to the north by Uldale Beck and is where wild fell ponies frequently graze.

Uldale Head to the west forms the northern flank of Carlin Gill and makes a good natural way to return to the start without any road-walking. All that is needed now is a short climb to the pile of stones on the summit and then gentle grassy slopes, becoming bracken-covered as they steepen by the side of Weasel Gill, lead easily back to the foot of Carlin Gill and the car.

The ravine of Black Force, Carlin Gill

20. The Langdale Skyline

Best maps: 1:40,000 Harvey Mountain Map
(Howgill Fells). Alternatively, OS Pathfinders
617 (Sedbergh and Baugh Fell) sheet SD
69/79 plus 607 (Tebay and Kirkby Stephen)
sheet NY 60/70; both are needed

Distance: About 14 miles/22.4km

Highest elevation reached: 2218ft/676m

Height gained: 2034ft/620m

Overall star rating: * * *

General level of exertion needed: Medium/high

Time for the round: About 6 hours

Terrain: Superb walking on grassy paths or open
high grassland but choose a fine day.

Geographically speaking, Nidderdale, Mallerstang and probably the Washburn valley are really part of what I might call the Greater Yorkshire Dales National Park and if half the Howgills are to be in it – as they are – then it seems mad to exclude the northern half, particularly since this superb round of the Langdale skyline is in the northern half . . .

Langdale is the longest of the northern Howgill valleys and the sources of the Langdale Beck rise from just below the highest point on these fells, The Calf. There are however several steep-sided subsidiary valleys whose streams all drain northwards to join Langdale Beck and these add greatly to the fine views, make navigation tricky in misty weather but also enable the route described to be easily shortened, by descending from the main ridge into them, if needed.

Start from Gaisgill (grid ref. 054640) reached by turning off the M6 at junction 38 and driving along the A685 signed for Brough. In about a mile and a half is a sign for Gaisgill on the right and a couple of cars can be parked near the telephone box just off the main road. Alternatively, drive the extra quarter of a mile to Longdale (as the OS somewhat perversely call it, when everything else is called Langdale) where there is plenty of parking space, then walk back.

Just beyond the telephone box, a gated farm track leads due south, through two gates between farm buildings at Ellergill, swings briefly left then right up a track between two widely-spaced walls, and heads south for the broad ridge whose high points are Rispa Pike and Uldale Head. When the track forks at a gate keep left, soon passing the farm at Long Gills, where there is a good view up the lower wooded part of Langdale itself, and then passing a ruined barn above the farm of Low Shaw. As the last intake walls curve

The head of Carlin Gill and Great Ulgill Beck seen from Uldale Head

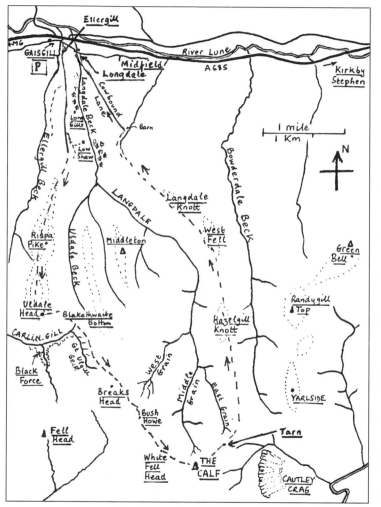

away towards Langdale, climb up a steeper slope, slightly west of south, on a much less used tractor track and fairly easy grassy walking soon leads to the semi-circular stone shelter on Rispa Pike.

This ridge continues to its high point at Uldale Head, about four miles from the start, with grand views into the deep ravine of Carlin Gill and a bird's eye view of Black Force. You must now lose some height, descending eastwards to the basin of Blakethwaite Bottom, from whence rise Uldale Beck flowing to the north and Carlingill Beck flowing west. The climb out is to the south-east, up grassy slopes (keeping just above the deeply eroded northern flank of Great Ulgill Beck) to reach the broad ridge of Wind Scarth and its high point at Breaks Head (grid ref. 654985, and not named on the OS 1:50,000 map). Here at last you are on the main summit ridge and a well-marked path now leads down to a little col (from whence the waters of West Grain drain north to Langdale) and up the other side to Bush Howe. Now the trig point on The Calf should be seen just right of the fan-shaped final gullies of Middle Grain, the head of Langdale itself, and an easy walk to White Fell Head and a final slope lead to The Calf.

I recall walking most of this fine ridge about twenty years ago, seeing no one else all day, sitting near the summit, listening to skylarks and counting the wild ponies I could see on a wide horizon. On a recent visit – a fine Sunday in March – I sat here, having passed about twenty ponies quietly grazing, one dead pony with white snow drifted against its black flanks and

eyeless sockets turned to the blue sky – and again having seen not a single human being.

A good path heads north-eastwards from The Calf but soon descends steeply towards the deep trench of Bowderdale, but this is not the way home. Before descending, however, this path passes a tiny tarn (sometimes dry) and it is essential to leave it here and head north, staying on the high ridge in order to keep the gills of East Grain on the left (west) hand and Bowderdale Beck on the right (east). For a hundred yards or so, the view ahead is obscured by rising ground, then the long ridge ahead can be seen, giving wonderful walking and gently undulating over Hazel-gill Knott and towards West Fell. Keep to the left (west) of this for the way now swings north-westwards, shadowing the curve of Langdale, with a last bit of rising ground (Langdale Knott) allowing a fine retrospective view of much of the walk. Long grassy slopes follow down to the intake walls and a rough track just outside them leads north now down a shallow gill to a ruined barn. Don't go down to Midfield from here for the initially walled Cowbound Lane leads unerringly down to the barns and houses of Langdale (or Longdale as the OS have it). Ten minutes or less westwards along the tarmac sees you back at Gaisgill.

Above left: *Wild ponies on the northern Howgills*

Above right: *Looking back up Langdale from Langdale Knott*

21. Mallerstang: The Crest and the Edge

Best maps: OS 1:50,000 Landranger 98
(Wensleydale and Upper Wharfedale) & 91
(Appleby-in-Westmorland): both are needed

Distance: About 13½ miles/21.6km

Highest elevation reached: 2326ft/709m

Height gained: 1640ft/500m

Overall star rating: **

General level of exertion needed: High

Time for the round: About 7 hours

Terrain: Largely trackless and sometimes very
rough going over peat moorland – but with
fine views. Not suitable in misty weather.

Unlike Wild Boar Fell, whose splendid wild edge coincides with the highest land, the equally fine edges on the eastern side of the valley do not, meaning that the walk is not quite so straightforward. The main walk described here is nevertheless a fine tramp.

Park at the north end of Mallerstang near Dalefoot, where the River Eden runs very close to the road and there is ample parking space on the grassy edge furthest from the river (grid ref. 781044). Alternatively there is a layby about two hundred yards further south.

To get going, a gate leads out onto open grassy slopes, then head south-east climbing steadily to reach some large piles of stones which look like mining or quarrying spoil, then up more slopes to Fair Hill where there are more of the same, as well as a couple of sheepfolds. In the same direction, the land leads higher yet to reach High Pike Hill and a broad expanse of half-stony, half-peaty wilderness which tilts gently towards Swaledale in the east. It is now easier going for a while, the route climbing gently up the west edge of this tilted plateau, though before long a dilemma needs resolving: to head for the sharp gritstone edges now becoming visible ahead or to go for the highest land, Hugh Seat, from whose large cairn Pen-y-ghent and Whernside can be seen at the head of Ribblesdale. In fact, the best bit of Mallerstang Edge is just west and below Hugh Seat so it is possible to go to the cairn on the latter, then, instead of immediately heading round a wide cirque towards Hugh Seat, descend a little to the Edge and walk along it to the three cairns on Hangingstone Scar, more stone men gazing to Wild Boar Fell over the stern valley below.

Now climb back and contour round the tiny stream

Pendragon Castle with Mallerstang Edge on the skyline

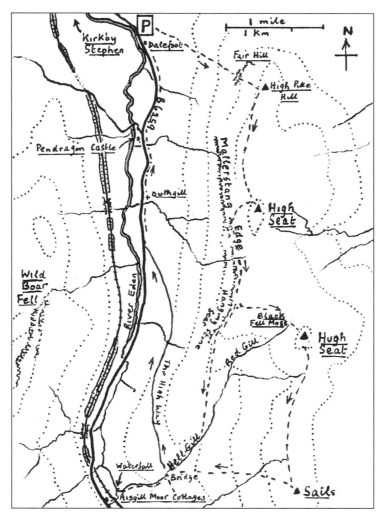

of Red Gill draining Black Fell Moss and so over to Hugh Seat. A wire fence here runs approximately along a boggy watershed where the rivers Ure and Eden rise just a few yards away from each other. Both flow west initially, though the Ure soon swings south and then east to the North Sea; the Eden flows west via Hell Gill. Climb the fence and head towards two stone men visible on the last high point of Sails. Lower down to the west stands another stone man, directly in line with Hell Gill Bridge, and a steady but rough descent leads to this, spanning a deep and – if you can get in a position to see it – spectacular limestone gorge down which the infant Eden thunders. This narrow bridge, just wide enough to take a horse and carriage (including the redoubtable Lady Anne Clifford's on her journeys between castles), is a crucial bit of The High Way, an ancient track used to link Wensleydale and Mallerstang. This track heading north under Mallerstang Edge returns to the road for a last tramp down it towards the start.

On the way, you will pass the unmistakable crumbling remains, beside the road, of Pendragon Castle. This is the reputed seat of Uther Pendragon, step-father of King Arthur of the Round Table, the stories of which held me spellbound for hours when I was an eight-year-old. This was once border country: Pendragon Castle was sacked by raiding Scots in the sixteenth century and then rebuilt a century later by the tireless Lady Anne Clifford (whose family owned Skipton Castle, still the finest medieval castle in the north of England). As you walk down the last stretch, on a straight bit of road about half a mile north of Pendragon Castle, look up to the skyline of Wild Boar Fell and (on a clear day) you should see the profile of a recumbent head gazing heavenwards. It is said that Sir Hugh de Morville, whose name is recalled in Hugh Seat (the top you recently traversed) and who was one of the murderers (under the King's orders) of Thomas à Becket in 1170 in Canterbury Cathedral, believed the profile was the face of Becket come to haunt him.

For a shorter round, instead of taking in Hugh Seat and Sails, you could descend south-south-westwards from Hangingstone Scar along a vague line of ledges leading towards Hell Gill, easily identified from above, and so pick up The High Way just north of the bridge. This will give you a walk of about 9 miles/ 14.4km, and take about five hours. If you did the main walk as described above but were able to arrange a pick-up at Aisgill Moor Cottages, you'd have a walk of about 8½ miles/13.6km and about 4½ hours long. *The* walk of Mallerstang, however (of about 17 miles/27.2km and 8½ hours), for which you would need a long clear day, would undoubtedly be the complete horseshoe. This climbs to Mallerstang Edge, descends to Hell Gill and Aisgill Moor Cottages for some welcome refreshment, then climbs to Swarth Fell Pike and Wild Boar Fell (*see* Walk 23). To complete the circuit, go beyond Little Fell and Green-law Rigg to the unfenced road which crosses the railway line above the tunnel at grid ref. 772032. This road crosses the River Eden close by Pendragon Castle and Dalefoot is then just a mile along the road.

The cairn on High Seat, Pen-y-ghent and Whernside in the distance

22.   The Nine Standards and Whitsundale

Best map: OS 1:50,000 Landranger 91 (Appleby-
   in-Westmorland area)

Distance: Max 9¼miles/14.8 km (see text)

Highest elevation reached: 2172ft/662m

Height gained: 860ft/262m

Overall star rating: */**

General level of exertion needed: Medium

Time for the round: About 4½ hours (see text)

Terrain: Mostly over peaty moorland paths;
   choose a clear day.
   NB The direct route from Lamps Moss is
   4 miles/6.4km, height gain 500ft/152m.

The great beacons or cairns of the Nine Standards excel in size and collective 'presence' even the finest at the head of Wensleydale. It's a wonder why they should be there at all, standing like sentries on a rampart at the northern edge of the Yorkshire Dales, gazing over the Stainmore Gap to the Northern Pennines. They demand to be visited – just because they are there; they are part of our landscape heritage. Unfortunately, some of the surrounding land is soft peat, suffering from erosion caused by feet. This will, in the long run, only be solved by laying stone slabs, the ancient packhorse 'causey-stones', across the vulnerable areas.

In the meantime, valiant attempts to 'manage' the erosion are taking place which, for practical purposes, means that the existing signposts are likely to be shifted from time to time. As a result, the original route I suggested in the first edition of this book, could now be misleading, so I have indicated the ways by which a walker may reach and return from the Nine Standards (excluding the approach from Kirkby Stephen via Faraday Gill).

The simplest route is a 'there and back' one using the public footpath from Lamps Moss, the highest point on the fell road (B6270) between Kirkby Stephen and Keld, at grid ref. 809042. This road is unenclosed, with numerous parking possibilities. A finger-post pointing north indicates the footpath, initially over limestone, but cairns and guide-posts soon mark a change of direction (to north-east) and a change to peatier moorland underfoot as Rigg Beck is crossed. From here on the path is clear, with continuing reassurance from guide-posts, climbing gradually to reach the broad, high plateau on the top of the fell. The trig point on Nine Standards Rigg appears ahead, but it is the sight of the Nine Standards themselves

The pillar on Coldbergh Edge and the view to High Pike Hill

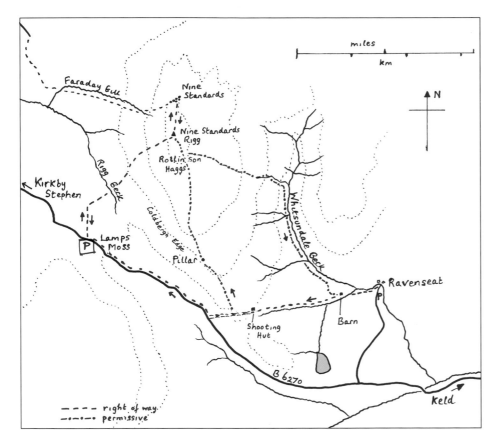

miles

km

N

Faraday Gill

Nine Standards

Nine Standards Rigg

Rollin' Son Haggs

Kirkby Stephen

Rigg Beck

Coldbergh Edge

Lamps Moss

P

Pillar

Whitsundale Beck

Ravenseat

P

Barn

Shooting Hut

B 6270

Keld

- - - - right of way
-·-·-·- permissive

orientation table indicating the peaks seen all round the points of the compass.

Having wandered around the Standards and admired the long-range views to the north, some of the magic of the place will have dissipated and you may well muse that they are just heaps of stones after all. But just wait until you have reversed your footsteps a little for the return journey; *then look back* and they will still be there, looming mysteriously on the skyline like ancient giants.

My original circular walk started in Ravenseat, the little hamlet to the north of the fell road (B6270) between Kirkby Stephen and Keld and since at least part of it is on an ancient public right of way, that part of it is unlikely to be altered. There is room for a few cars just at the side of the old bridge there at grid ref. 863033. A ladder-stile leads over the wall, heading just south of west, up Whitsundale Beck, but as soon as a barn is passed, take the left-hand branch, keeping in the same westerly direction alongside Ney Gill.

The path now leads up the right-hand side of the gill which is wide, wet and basically boring but leads past a sheepfold and some grouse butts to reach a shooting-hut. Just beyond this a firm jeep track continues westwards (and in half a mile joins the B6270 road) but in 300 yards, just round a slight bend, you may find a signpost marked 'Coast to Coast' and pointing north to a tall pillar of rock on the skyline (Coldbergh Edge) ahead. Unfortunately, it is only a

that sets your feet scampering a bit faster to reach them; they are so large that it is not easy to realise that they are in fact still five hundred yards away. On the way, you pass a separate big cairn, with a brass

The Nine Standards

permissive path and part of the 'management' might involve it being closed. If it is still there you may safely assume that the route is still open and guide-posts will lead you round the morasses of Rollinson Haggs and onto the plateau to the Nine Standards. If not, the only legal suggestion I can make is that you continue along the jeep track to the B6270, turn right and walk beside it for 1½ miles/2.4km (it is undulating, with little height gain) as far as Lamps Moss and there pick up the footpath described above to reach the Nine Standards.

For the return to Ravenseat, there has been for some time now a permissive path reversing the last 400 yards SSE from the trig point on Nine Standards Rigg and then heading ESE for about 1 mile/1.6km to join and follow Whitsundale Beck. Reaching intake walls it then turns sharp right (south) to the ruined barn and rejoins the last bit of the public path back to Ravenseat. This route was marked with signposts (and shown on the 1:25000 OS Outdoor Leisure 33 Coast to Coast Walk map) and if the posts are still there, just follow them back to the hamlet.

109

23.   Swarth Fell and Wild Boar Fell

Best map: OS 1:25,000 Pathfinder 617 (Sedbergh
     and Baugh Fell) sheet SD 69/79. Also on
     Harvey Mountain Map 1:40,000 (Howgill
     Fells) and OS 1:50,000 Landranger 98
     (Wensleydale & Upper Wharfedale)

Distance: About 8 miles/12.8km

Highest elevation reached: 2323ft/708m

Height gained: 1109ft/338m

Overall star rating: * * *

General level of exertion needed: High

Time for the round: About 4 hours

Terrain: Rough grassy moor on ascent; fair path
     along the edges; rough descent.

Both Swarth Fell and Wild Boar Fell present their finest features, their sharp gritstone nebs and edges, to Mallerstang. My own first view of them was from the window of a steam-train on the famous Settle to Carlisle run, where the view from Aisgill Moor on the highest point of the line is the culmination of a breathtaking journey. I hopped up and down with excitement: what a delight for a fellwalker,

especially with its advantage of starting at about 1200 feet above sea level!

There's an old quarry (with a waterfall tumbling into it) just before reaching Cotegill Bridge on the B6259 Sedbergh to Kirkby Stephen road (grid ref. 774969) but the best parking spot is at Aisgill Moor Cottages at grid ref. 777963, because you'll find there a wonderful welcome and a super cup of tea just when you need it most. The cottages were originally built for railway workers, like those at Ribblehead, and there's a bridge over the railway just a few paces south of them. Across the bridge, dividing it into two halves but each being wide enough to take a cart, can be seen the footings of a now demolished high brick wall which was built because of the mutual hatred of two farmers who farmed sheep on both sides of the line but couldn't stand the sight of each other. The one place where they had to pass was the bridge, hence the wall.

More or less opposite the bridge at a gate onto the moor is a footpath sign for Garsdale and this path heads south. Swarth Fell, however, is due west so, although there's no path, go west to join and then follow the line taken by Smithy Gill. This leads over tussocky grass moor until, after a short, sharp haul to several cairns on Swarth Fell Pike, you continue just a little further to reach the southern end of the line of gritstone crags on Swarth Fell, and a wonderful view.

Snow blowing off Swarth Fell, looking south

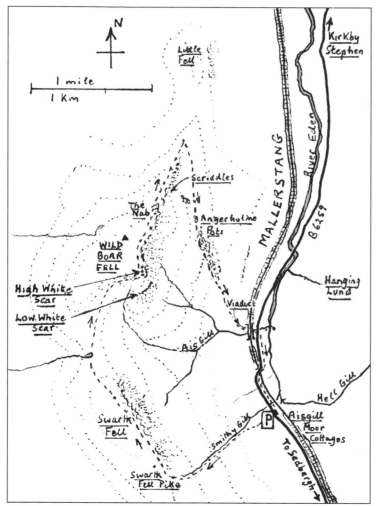

Baugh Fell to the south-west looks huge and flat; Wild Boar Fell, seen across the combe of Aisgill, shows two nebs from here, and the cluster of stone men on High White Scar can usually be clearly seen. There are more cairns at the northern end of the edge on Swarth Fell then this fades into the hillside and a faint path leads down northwards beside the wall to a little tarn on the hause. As the wall curves away west towards the Howgills and a view of Cautley Spout, the path climbs the far side of the hollow, avoiding Low White Scar and heading directly for the largest cairn amongst the five stone men on High White Scar which stare across the valley of Mallerstang. This is an impressive place, looking across a deep crag-fringed combe with a jumble of gritstone boulders below to another cairn on The Nab beyond.

Hoping for a photograph from here I nearly froze solid one winter's day. I hid behind the biggest cairn whilst the wind blew snow horizontally outwards into the void. I didn't bother going to the summit trig point, left behind the Celtic chieftain's tumulus on The Nab and, keeping north down the continuing edge above Scriddles, reached a little circular stone shelter. I then realised that Freddie, one of my dogs, was wandering in circles and getting perilously close to the edge. He came towards the sound of my voice and I was then able to clear enough ice from around his eyes for him to see.

The little shelter is at a low point along the edge and is the best place to descend, though steeply, towards a field of grass-covered limestone clints to the

Wild Boar Fell seen from Swarth Fell

south-east (a little north of the line of shake-holes of Angerholme Pots which stand out clearly from above). The great ice cap of the last Ice Age, some ten thousand years ago, was centred on Wild Boar Fell and Baugh Fell and although it is clear that the gritstone boulders below The Nab obviously collapsed from the edge, there are others on the limestone pavement here which are too huge and too far away from The Nab. To me, they look more like the famous 'erratic' boulders of Norber, carried and then deposited by moving ice.

A solid wall runs along the edge of this limestone scarp from north to south and is a perfect guide now with a sheep path alongside it, towards the Aisgill viaduct. If the weather is or has been recently very wet, you may have a good view of the waterfall of Hanging Lund on the side of the valley opposite, where a beck on the moor above sinks into limestone and then reappears, spouting out from a hole below the level of the scar in a dramatic cascade.

All that remains is just under a mile of road, and that tea.

24. Grisedale, Hell Gill and the High Way

Best map: OS 1:50,000 Landranger 98
(Wensleydale & Upper Wharfedale) although
most of the walk is on OS 1:25,000 Pathfinder
617 (Sedbergh and Baugh Fell) sheet SD
69/79

Distance: About 12½ miles/20km

Highest elevation reached: 1640ft/500m

Height gained: 942ft/287m

Overall star rating: **

General level of exertion needed: Medium

Time for the round: About 5–6 hours

Terrain: An undulating walk over high moorland,
mostly on good or fair paths though some
stretches can be wet and rough. Some superb
views.

This most interesting walk links the heads of three valleys: Garsdale, Mallerstang and Wensleydale and an ideal start, seeing all the most scenic parts of that wonderful journey, can be made by taking the Settle to Carlisle railway to Garsdale Head Station and alighting there. Or you may go by car and park near the station on the side of the minor road (the 'Coal Road') leading over to Dentdale (grid ref. 786919).

From the station, walk downhill to the main A684 road and a finger-post and slit-stile opposite, signed for 'Grisedale and Flust', with another stile ahead up the field. To the left is the little waterfall of Clough Force but the faint path leads north-westwards up the hillside, to pass by the lonely farmhouse at Blake Mire. From here you have a first view into Grisedale, a high, remote hollow between the wild reaches of Baugh Fell and Swarth Fell. The valley was once the home of a dozen families until the economic blizzards of the 1930s forced almost complete abandonment of their farms. Finger-posts point the way to the white farmhouse at Moor Rigg and then, crossing the tarmac road (which ends just a few yards beyond here), a further finger-post ('FP East House 2 via Round Ing') signs a way down to the Grisedale Beck and past the first of a series of ruined farmsteads. Further on, a stone footbridge leads to the sad and dilapidated farmsteads of East Scale and West Scale, now silent and deserted. Return to the stone foot-bridge and cross over it to where a nearby finger-post points up the slope to Round Ing, where even the trees are giving up the struggle against the elements and little more than a heap of stones remains.

Grisedale, with Swarth Fell on the horizon

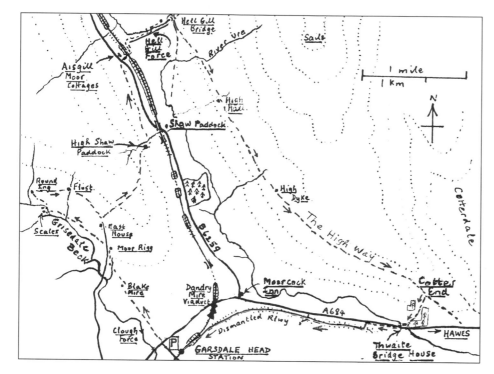

down towards some obvious (unoccupied) farm buildings at High Shaw Paddock where a right of way path leads parallel to the lonely road and railway. This emerges by a gate opposite the delightful tea-rooms at Aisgill Moor Cottages, the highest point on the Settle to Carlisle line.

Bill and Pauline Hasted who run the tea-rooms told me a tale about how the local farmer eventually got fed up with the steam-railway enthusiasts taking pictures from this spot and continually knocking stones off his walls and not replacing them. One day therefore, he waited until all the long lenses were set up on tripods and the train was almost in sight, then drove his slurry-waggon round the field, providing an environmentally-friendly fragrance.

Cross the railway bridge and follow the track curving round just above Hell Gill Force and up past the farm to where Hell Gill Bridge spans the extraordinarily deep and narrow gulf of Hell Gill itself. Here the infant River Eden has carved deeply into the limestone to create a gorge which is almost hidden below rampant vegetation. For an adventurous enthusiast not frightened of a wetting, this can give the finest gill-scramble in the whole of the Dales.

The old 'High Way' now gives the line of the walk, but it is easy to go wrong here. So, from the bridge follow the obvious green way going due south but only for 200 yds; now turn off it, climbing gently, along a faint path (bearing 150 degrees magnetic) heading towards a wall-corner with a gate. Keep just outside the wall on its left side and very shortly cross a little

Turn south-east now and follow signs to Flust, then a good cart track leads to East House. Just before reaching the farm, head north-east up the fellside which forms a long spur down from Swarth Fell since this needs to be crossed to get over to Mallerstang. It can be fairly rough going for a short way (there's a path on the map but not on the ground), curving round to the north over the broad crest and then

gill down which flows the infant River Ure, with a little clump of ash trees beside it. Cross open pasture to another wall-corner; again keep on the left outside it and continue to the ruins of High Hall. The High Way now gives splendid high-level walking on springy grass along a series of broad sloping limestone shelves, crossing several little gills and passing more ruins, but always just outside the intake wall. The last ruin, that of High Dyke, was once a drover's pub in the days when the High Way was the main road.

Continue to Cotter End which overlooks the head of Wensleydale. On the steep descent, pass a lime-kiln and turn through the right-hand of the two gates just below it. Go steeply down the field to the south-west and towards the top corner of an L-shaped conifer wood, passing another little wood on the left on the way down. A ladder-stile leads into another field and a descent towards Thwaite Bridge House; to the left of this, a final ladder-stile leads through some trees to the bridge itself. Turn right (west) up the main road. In about three hundred yards a track on the left leads directly onto the line of the dismantled Wensleydale railway. This gives very pleasant walking and an easy return to Garsdale Head Station.

Hell Gill Force,
Mallerstang

117

The hill of Kisdon and Thwaite village, Swaledale

PART THREE

Wensleydale and Swaledale

25. Aysgarth Falls and Penhill

Best map: OS 1:25,000 Yorkshire Dales (Northern & Central areas)

Distance: About 10 miles/16km

Highest elevation reached: 1726ft/526m

Height gained: 1168ft/356m

Overall star rating: **/***

General level of exertion needed: Medium

Time for the round: About 5 hours

Terrain: Mostly on good or fair paths, even on the high moor.

Penhill with its beacon dominates the skyline of lower Wensleydale and begs to be climbed, while the Aysgarth Falls are rightly famous and have to be seen. This excellent walk, marred only by two short road sections, links them by way of the Templars' Chapel ruins and the fine waterfall and attractive village of West Burton.

Park at Aysgarth in the Yorkshire Dales National Park car park on the north side of the River Ure at grid ref. 012887. If you haven't seen the Falls before, follow the signs from the car park to view the two-tiered cascade of the Middle Force, then back to see the Upper Force from the road bridge. Now cross the bridge, go up the steps towards St Andrew's Church and head east along the far (south) side of the church; a couple of stiles quickly lead to rolling green pastures along the riverside and, very soon, a fine view of the Lower Force where the Ure pours through a little gorge and then along a level limestone pavement. Penhill is on the eastern skyline, a series of limestone shelves capped by a flattened gritstone dome.

Markers soon lead the little-used path away from the river to join the A684 just before Hestholme Bridge. Walk east along the verge and slightly uphill until you reach a sign for 'Templars' Chapel ½', opposite a strange octagonal building which is set behind a stone wall on the left. A cart track leads up on to the first limestone scar, and then over a stile are the ruins of the Knights Templars' Chapel, built about AD 1200. The Templars had been the most powerful of the three great military Orders which had emerged out of the Crusades, the others being the Teutonic Order and the Knights of St John of Jerusalem. The tiny stone coffins seen here are a link with a fascinating past.

Now take the track signed for 'Nossill Lane via Langthwaite Lane' which climbs to the south-east and

Aysgarth Middle Force in flood

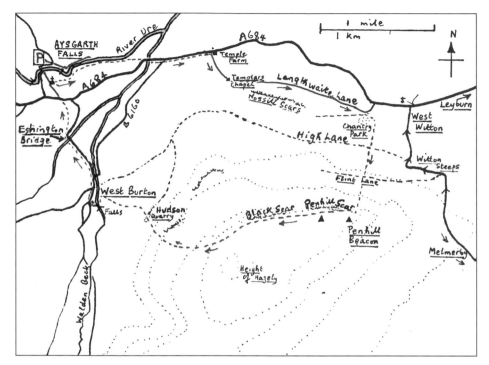

Go south-eastwards across the second field to a barn, then left (east) along a walled lane for 75 paces to a slit-stile and here turn sharp right (south). Continue in a direct line for the beacon on Penhill seen up the slope ahead. High Lane is crossed using stiles on each side; higher up you pass a ruined barn and then cross Flint Lane, also by stiles. High up on the moor now, walk alongside the last wall, past old quarry tips, to emerge on the shoulder of the east ridge at a gate. Here you meet the footpath used by those faint souls who have parked their cars at the top of Witton Steeps and just walked up the last bit. A last short climb brings you to the beacon – although not the top, for the trig point is further on behind a wall. Not that it matters since the views are infinitely better from here. A hundred yards or so to the west is a heap of stones, a tumulus, reputedly the grave of an Iron Age chieftain; this looks out over a splendid panorama of Wensleydale and, nearer, to the fine crags of Penhill Scar. The Scar gives the line of advance now, heading west on a well-marked path and keeping close to the edge, beyond more crags on Black Scar, until the curve of the moor, with the wall just below, begins to swing south.

You could now, if you choose, carry on southwards a little further to pick up the obvious track that descends westwards down Thupton Gill to West Burton. Although you may well find a better one, the best way off the moor top that I found was over a stile, where there is a bit of fencing instead of wall, and then down a grass rake, heading west until there is a

the next limestone shelf below Nossill Scars. A path leads over open pasture and then into the walled Langthwaite Lane which, for fifty yards, is almost overgrown with blackthorn; the path continues pleasantly until the Chantry Park caravan site is reached. Keep on the lane a little further until it curves towards West Witton, then take a signed path ('Moor Bank ½') on the right which leads through the caravan site.

View towards Coverdale from the beacon on Penhill

suddenly steeper descent to the disused Hudson Quarry. A signed footpath now leads to zigzags down a limestone scarp and across the lower fields to the elegant stone footbridge, gorge and waterfalls of the Walden Beck at West Burton.

The return to Aysgarth is straightforwardly along the road following the river, turning along Eshington Lane (the footpath is beside the road on the other side of the wall) as far as Eshington Bridge. Here, where the road swings sharply right, you may either follow it to join the A684 and so return to Aysgarth; or, much better, leave the road and make a last little climb up the fields to the NNW on a track and footpath (signed) enabling you to cut the corner and reach the A684. Take the track on the other side of the road; this leads past the vicarage and so back to the church at Aysgarth from where it is an easy return to the car park on the other side of the river.

26. Waldendale and Harland Hill

Best map: OS 1:25,000 Yorkshire Dales (Northern
& Central areas)

Distance: About 8 miles/12.9km

Highest elevation reached: 1755ft/535m

Height gained: 1066ft/325m

Overall star rating: */**

General level of exertion needed: Medium

Time for the round: About 4 hours

Terrain: Good paths except on Harland Hill itself,
which is tussocky.

Although Waldendale has two metalled roads running along its length, neither of them continues beyond the head of the dale, for Buckden Pike effectively blocks any further progress. There is consequently no through traffic and the dale is particularly tranquil and secluded. This walk leads up on to the high land dividing Coverdale from Waldendale, where there are some fine views, then goes for a pleasant ramble up Waldendale itself.

The best start for the walk is from Cote Bridge where there is room for a few cars (grid ref. 018855).

Walk south for a few paces past Cote Farm and then take the wide walled lane on the left (east) leading up Thupton Gill; you will pass the remains of a stumpy chimney and its flue, all that are now left of a little lead-smelting mill. Although steep and stony to begin with, the surface underfoot soon improves; when the walls disappear, the track makes a wide swing to the right to avoid the steepest part of the gill and then contours back towards its head, with good views towards West Burton and out over Wensleydale. The hause between Harland Hill and Height of Hazely/ Penhill is soon reached at a wall running along the summit ridge. The track beyond continues through a gate and down to Carlton in Coverdale but just before reaching it, turn right (SSW) along a less well-defined track over ground marked as 'Bleaberry Pots' on the OS map. This soon peters out and leaves you picking a slanting line over tousle-headed grass tussocks towards the summit wall, to reach a sheepfold in the wall-corner. Use this to cross over to the east side of the wall and stay alongside it over the unmarked top of the hill when long-range views of Great Whernside at the head of Coverdale and of Buckden Pike at the head of Waldendale should be visible.

I can't recall where I read it, but I believe the last wild boar in England was hunted and killed in Waldendale and, seeing from here how secluded and

*Harland Hill from Dove
Scar*

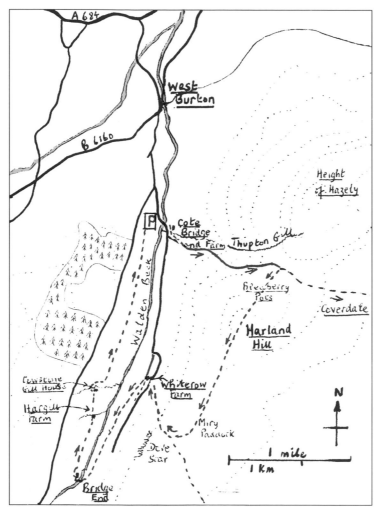

sheltered it is, I don't find it difficult to believe, particularly when the woods and forests were more extensive than now.

The wall gives a steady descent now to a broad and peaty hause and a gate near the place on the OS map named 'Miry Paddock' enables you to return easily to the western side; then continue downhill and meet with the grassy track that winds over Fleensop Moor to Coverdale. This quickly leads in turn to a gateway through the intake wall near Dove Scar and so to the road.

Turn left here, where there is a sign 'F.P. Bridgend 1' and take the track as far as Whiterow Farm. When level with its last barn, leave the track and slant across the field towards another barn and a gate with a yellow arrow. From here the footpath gives a charming ramble up Waldendale at a level well below the tarmac road, descending to the stream at Bridge End (where the farm has been re-named). Across the footbridge, pass to the left of the farm to a slit-stile in a wall to reach the farm track beyond. Now go NNE across the meadow on a faint path to the first of a series of slit-stiles and gates. You cross the beck just before Hargill Farm and then finger-post and other signs lead you to and around Cowstone Gill House and a delightful stretch of easy walking back to Cote Bridge.

Looking down Thupton Gill towards Aysgarth and Wensleydale

27. Drumaldrace from Marsett

Best map: OS 1:25,000 Yorkshire Dales (Northern & Central areas)

Distance: About 8 miles/12.8km

Highest elevation reached: 2014ft/614m

Height gained: 1145ft/349m

Overall star rating: */**

General level of exertion needed: Medium

Time for the round: About 3½–4 hours

Terrain: A mixture of open moorland grass pasture, good tracks and high rough moorland.

The becks flowing down Cragdale, Raydale and Bardale drain into the largest natural lake in the Dales, Semer Water, which was formed by glacial debris damming the outlet from a cirque of high and lonely fells. An old Roman road marches out of Bainbridge – now a delightful little village but once the site of an important fort – straight up the edge of the northern arm of the cirque, staying as long as possible on the highest land above the forests that covered these islands before they were progressively cleared for grain and sheep pastures. The walk climbs up to the Roman road and returns down the wild gill of Bardale, giving on a fine day some of the best views in upper Wensleydale.

The most interesting way to reach Marsett is to drive south-east out of Bainbridge on the A684, cross the River Bain and take the first turn sharp right (south-west) and uphill, taking the right fork along Blean Lane. This gives a good view over Semer Water from its east side and an equally good one to the fells to the west, where the Roman road (the Cam High Road) traverses the skyline. Now turn sharply downhill to pass close by Semer Water's edge and then the road climbs above its north-west shore on the way to Marsett. The huge limestone boulder, part of the glacier debris, by the little bay at the north end of the lake and known as the Carlow Stone, has been variously described as a site for pagan human sacrifice and also as a missile hurled by a giant at the Devil (see also Walk 28). The Devil, on the the side of the lake, grabbed for a similar sized one to hurl back but the one he seized was too heavy and it slipped from his fingers. Sure enough, on the far side is a huge boulder with five deep scars gouged into it by devilish claws. I don't suppose you'll hear any church bells ringing in the village now sunk below the water, although some claim to have heard them.

The Cam High Road looking towards Bainbridge

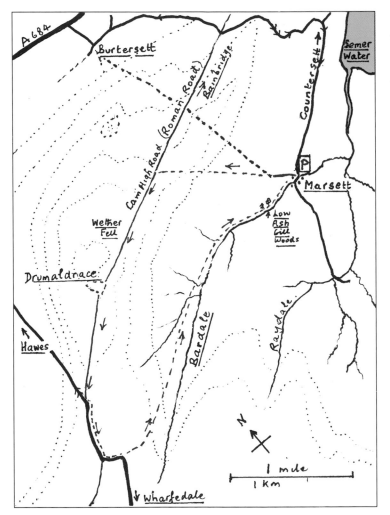

Park where you can in Marsett; there's space for a couple of cars just before crossing the bridge by the telephone box (grid ref. 903863), then find the finger-post for 'Burtersett 2, Hawes 3' which you passed just yards before reaching the phone box. This points uphill along a farm track, through two gates and leads into a farmyard at 'Bella or Knight Close' (grid ref. 899864). As you enter it, immediately climb a little bank on the right (which encloses the farm-yard) to a gate in the wall (no sign) and climb north-west across the field to a stile (no path either, but it is the right way). Now go steeply uphill, still going north-west, to another stile and another field, keeping to the right of a shallow gill. Looking back, Semer Water can be seen now, backed by Addle-brough's flat top and sharp distinctive neb. Another wall is ahead, and then a tiny sheepfold just over a rise has gates on both sides; so go through these and on to a sort of tractor-track which leads firmly in the right direction towards Wether Hill now clearly seen as a long hump of high land ahead. The track ends at a fenced off sheepfold, but the wall side quickly leads uphill to a junction with the Cam High Road.

Turn left uphill here and now it is easy walking for a while up the old Roman way, walled on both sides and heading for Ribblehead and Ingleton. Near the top, the Cam High Road kinks left and reaches a gate, then contours just under the highest land so that to visit Drumaldrace, the highest point, you have to leave it for a brief climb over rough moor to the lonely gritstone cairn on the flattish top. All around is a

Beggarman's Road descending to Hawes; Cam High Road on right

complete circle of wild moorland, with the Howgills and Wild Boar Fell distinctive to the north-west. Returning to the Cam High Road, it is still easy going but then traces of old tarmac appear as it dips down to join the metalled Beggarman's Road coming from Hawes over Oughtershaw Moss to Beckermonds at the head of Wharfedale. Now you can understand why Wether Hill is a popular launching site for hang-gliders.

Fortunately, it's not far along the tarmac, bearing left (south-east) at the junction towards Oughtershaw and then turning through the first gate on the left where a tractor-track curves down towards Bardale. The right of way path leads down the slopes, initially above the Bardale Beck but shortly alongside the tumbling waters, with some fairly boggy passages as you lose height. You'll notice the transition from gritstone to limestone as you pass a little cut-back limestone shelf with a waterfall and then Low Ash Gill Woods come into view ahead. Here the stream runs through a delightful little gorge, whose banks would make an enchanting picnic place, after which a few slit-stiles lead easily back alongside the beck to Marsett.

131

28. Addlebrough and the Devil's Stone

Best map: OS 1:25,000 Yorkshire Dales (Northern & Central areas)

Distance: About 5½ miles/8.8km

Highest elevation reached: 1562ft/476m

Height gained: 742ft/226m

Overall star rating: */**

General level of exertion needed: Medium

Time for the round: About 2½–3 hours

Terrain: Good moorland path on the outward leg; easy grass moor on the return. The odd wall and fence need to be climbed.

Addlebrough's sharp neb and flat top are like the prow of some great aircraft carrier surging into Wensleydale and, like Penhill, are eye-catching from many angles. If, like me, you have an irresistible urge to climb to the top of places like that, to get the eagle's eye view, to soar above the plodding valleys where we have to spend so much of our lives, then it won't take much to persuade you to set off. It's a splendid viewpoint and a place charged with a bit of magic, but when I went up there, I had no map and was quite unaware that there was no right-of-way or permissive path. You can still get a decent walk, however, going round it and the views are often better from the flanks than from the tops themselves.

Park in Thornton Rust (grid ref. 975888), where there's plenty of space in the quiet main street, then go south-westwards up the lane opposite the Village Institute. This leads across a little stream (ford), round a bend to the right, another back left and then (with a bridleway sign on the corner) back right again, climbing up above Thornton Rust now, with fine views across Wensleydale. When this walled lane runs into a pasture, a bridleway sign points south-west across it to a ladder-stile over a wall at a slightly higher level, and then across a grassy moor. Addlebrough will be clearly in view now and the track leads towards the hause or shoulder to the left (west) of the summit plateau, crosses a little depression and then, as it approaches a cross wall, turns right through a gate in a wall running round the base of the hill and through another gate in a wall running down from the plateau above. The track (now ill-defined) continues to meet the metalled Carpley Green Road descending to Bainbridge and that's the way to go.

I recall going uphill alongside the wall after the second gate to a little stony edge, memorable because just beyond it are several vaguely circle-shaped

Wensleydale seen from near Thornton Rust

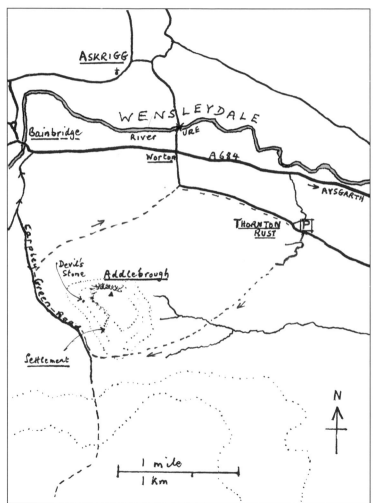

jumbles of stones and a nearby cairn which is the site of the 'settlement' marked on the map (grid ref. 950875). It is known that the Brigantes' chief Venutius, some nineteen hundred years ago, tried to prevent the northern march of the Roman legionaries by building defensive earthworks on passes such as that at Tor Dike which leads over Park Rash from Kettlewell in Wharfedale to Coverdale. He built a massive fort at Stanwick, a fort on top of Ingleborough and apparently one on top of Addlebrough. Perhaps these jumbled stones had something to do with that?

I certainly felt as though I were in touch with the distant past as I stood there alone with just the lapwings and the curlews crying down the wind and a view to the east down Wensleydale to Penhill, with its ancient chieftain's grave on the summit. The magic wasn't over yet though for somewhere here I knew was the 'Devil's Stone'. I continued towards the main edge away to the left which begins gently enough, just a little scarp emerging from the moor, but it gathers height and definition as it goes. I walked along it, expecting to find the Devil's Stone below the prow somewhere. It is below but it is to one side and, although limestone, it is massive and mostly smooth, apparently having no other relationship to the crumbling and fractured square-edged little blocks of the edge itself. Legend has it that the Devil and a giant threw stones at each other hereabouts (and there are another couple of stones on the edge of Semer Water – *see* Walk 27 – which is in view to the west) and this

Addlebrough from the hillside above Semer Water

must have been one of those; the only clear markings on it, down one side, are a long vertical mark and a horizontal one across it, with three other vertical marks above the horizontal line. I first thought it looked like an odd-shaped cross but then I realised that it was clearly where the Devil had seized the stone in his great claws and the single deep gouge was that of his thumb while the other four marks were those of his fingers . . .

I scrambled to a point on the top of the prow, which is about 25 feet high here, with the land dropping steeply below; a marvellous viewpoint – or observation post for a chieftain of old.

Retracing my steps past the jumbled stones of the settlement and the gate, I soon picked up the path again leading to the metalled Carpley Green Road. A gentle ramble along this for about three quarters of a mile soon brought me to the point where, just before it goes more steeply downhill at grid ref. 936884, I found the path leading north-east gently down Worton Pasture to the road. It was then just a stroll back to the car in Thornton Rust.

29.   Askrigg's Waterfalls and Beyond

Best map: OS 1:25,000 Yorkshire Dales (Northern & Central areas)

Distance: About 8¾ miles/14km

Highest elevation reached: 1165ft/355m

Height gained: 420ft/128m

Overall star rating: */**

General level of exertion needed: Low

Time for the round: About 3½–4 hours

Terrain: On good paths throughout.

This attractive low-level walk visits two fine water-falls, traverses a grassy shelf below Ellerkin Scar and returns to Askrigg from Woodhall along the line of the disued railway. Even on a wet day it has attractions, and the waterfalls will be that much better.

Park in Askrigg, usually possible near or in front of St Oswald's Church (grid ref. 948911). This dates from 1175, although later alterations have changed it substantially and its solid buttresses and crenellated roofline are very much in keeping with the unusual three-storey houses in the main street. Askrigg

enjoyed a position as a centre of trade and industry in Elizabethan times, long before the Wensleydale railway line, opened in 1877, enabled the dairy products of Wensleydale to become better known to the wider world. The cobbles, the village pump and the old cross in the square give an air of tradition and continuity, although the darker side of that is also recalled by the iron bull-ring found (if not beneath a parked car) just a few feet away from the pump towards the main street; this was used for the 'sport' of bull-baiting.

On a corner of the church wall is a sign 'Footpath to Mill Gill Force' which leads down a lane going north-west and past the school, to skirt Mill Gill House. Here the path is signed across a field on small paving-stones, crosses to the west bank of Mill Gill and then leads up the top left side of the gill, between an enclosing wall and a steep, wooded slope. When the path forks, the right one leads to the wooded amphitheatre where Mill Gill Force tumbles over a limestone lip in a series of steps with an overall height of about 60ft/20m.

There is no escape from here so retreat to the fork in the path and this time take the left path which is signed for Whitfield Gill; continue up the top edge of the gill and over a couple of stiles to a signpost for 'Askrigg via Low Straights Lane' across the beck.

Ellerkin Scar, Wensleydale, seen from near Woodhall

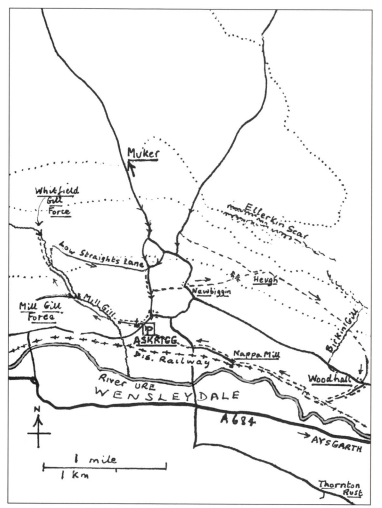

Muker

Whitfield
Gill
Force

Ellerkin Scar

Low Straights Lane

Heugh

Newbiggin

Mill Gill
Force

Mill Gill

P

ASKRIGG

Birkin Gill

Dis. Railway

Nappa Mill

Woodhall

River URE
WENSLEYDALE

A684

→ AYSGARTH

N

1 mile

1 km

Thornton
Rust

Don't take this but continue up the gill to another fork and signpost where one sign repeats the previous message while the left-hand sign says 'Whitfield Force only'. Follow this path in order to see the cascade which has an uninterrupted fall but over a wider front than Mill Gill's. It is possible to creep behind the waterfall, but it is not nearly so easy as at Hardraw and I found it very nerve-wracking; my two little dogs watched with justified trepidation and refused to follow. Sometimes they've more sense than me.

Return to the last sign 'FP Askrigg via Low Straights' and this time cross the stream by the footbridge and follow the path which leads up the top edge of the ravine on the other side and enters the walled Low Straights Lane. It is now easy walking back towards Askrigg, turning downhill on reaching the tarmac but then, as the 'Askrigg' boundary sign is reached, turn off left (east) at a footpath sign which points across pastures to the hamlet of Newbiggin. The footpath is signed again just across the tiny green and leads up a field, slanting gently towards and through a little mixed wood, then up to the top right-hand corner of the next field just above the disused quarry at Heugh. Here a walled bridleway is met (and a sign 'Castle Bolton 5¼') and this leads gently uphill, with the crags of Ellerkin Scar visible on the skyline above, quickly becoming a grassy track leading south-eastwards along a broad grassy ledge bounded by a line of shake-holes.

This is easy and very pleasant walking with comforting signposts, then Birkin Gill Beck is crossed at a tiny ford and the track winds down to the village of Woodhall. Cross the road and take the lane opposite signed 'Woodhall only' which leads through the village, becomes a track and reaches the line of the disused railway at a little cutting through the embankment. Go through the cutting and the path then runs along below the far side of the embankment for a couple of fields (signed) and then, having crossed to the north side, goes along its top. It is flat, grassy, easy and straight, while the river meanders in wide loops nearby. At Nappa Mill, the path along the embankment is blocked and leaves it to join the eastern end of a tarmac lane which is now taken towards Askrigg. When this lane meets the road there is a slit-stile directly opposite and a good path, signed 'F.P. Askrigg ½', leads across meadows to an extremely narrow walled lane which emerges exactly opposite the church.

Mill Gill Force, Askrigg

30. Pike Hill from Hawes

Best map: OS 1:50,000 Landranger 98 (Wensleydale & Upper Wharfedale)

Distance: About 7 miles/11.2km

Highest elevation reached: 1755ft/535m

Height gained: About 984ft/300m

Overall star rating: * *

General level of exertion needed: Medium

Time for the round: About 4 hours

Terrain: Some tarmac, but mostly on good paths over limestone. Guide-posts mark the route when it is unclear on the ground.

Most of the high gritstone moorland at the head of Wensleydale can give very soggy tramping but this walk over Stags Fell and Pike Hill is almost all on limestone, giving a grand walk with fine views over Hawes and Wensleydale.

Starting from the car park at the National Park Centre at the east end of Hawes (grid ref. 876898), turn north-west onto the Sedbusk-Hardraw road and follow it, cutting off a corner by a stone-flagged path on the left, signed for the Pennine Way. Rejoining the road, cross the River Ure by the double-arched Haylands Bridge and then take another footpath on the left, also signed 'Pennine Way' which leads, with more flags, to Hardraw, emerging directly opposite the Green Dragon pub.

Entrance to Hardraw Force is only through the pub's premises and there is a small charge, but it is well worth it to see England's highest unbroken waterfall above ground. This amazing cascade pours over the lip of an amphitheatre whose softer rocks have been eaten away at the base so that it is possible to walk behind the waterfall; the noise is deafening. The acoustics are so good that the long tradition of holding brass band contests here was revived by the present landlords of the pub in 1989 and they have been held ever since then, on the second Sunday in September each year. If ever a modern stuntman offered to do what the Frenchman Blondin did here in 1883, to walk a tight-rope suspended across the amphitheatre – and stop to cook an omelette half way across! – I reckon the pub would run out of beer.

After visiting the Force, turn left immediately on leaving the front entrance of the pub to find a footpath signed between the buildings which climbs up the field behind them (north-east) over stone flags and steps. This path becomes a track beyond the farm of West House, leading to the road connecting

Looking south-east across Wensleydale from High Clint

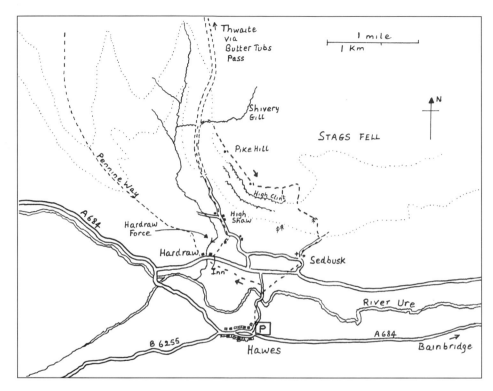

flags and despatched them in great quantities by rail from Hawes until the 1890s.

Above the cattle-grid the road is unenclosed, the angle eases and in about 15 minutes you reach a point where the beck of Shivery Gill is bridged by a culvert; here a finger-post reading 'Bridleway' points directly up the fellside on the right to where the gill can be seen cutting the skyline. Just left of the gill itself a jeep track climbs the short distance to another guide-post which points south to another on the far side of the little ravine. These are just the first of several more such posts which now guide you along a series of limestone edges, with fine views to the west over Fossdale, to reach a group of cairns which mark Pike Hill. Heading for another guide-post seen ahead and keeping SSW, the path becomes increasingly clear and turns into a lovely green way across a broad grassy limestone plateau.

This track bypasses a large cairn, with two more nearby, on the east end of High Clint, but do divert to them for more grand views. The continuation of this track now leads due east but again it is well worthwhile leaving it briefly, after about a quarter-mile, and swing right (south) to the east end of High Clint; from here you will enjoy a stunning view down Wensleydale.

Regaining the track, follow it to where it turns slightly downhill and reaches another guide-post. This time the direction is south and a path leads easily and then increasingly steeply down to a gate in the intake wall. From here the path slants south-east

Wensleydale with Swaledale by way of the Butter Tubs Pass. Walk left up the road as it gains height, to cross a cattle-grid where there are white gates on each side. On this ascent you can look across the flank of Stags Fell, on the right, and see the terraces, spoil heaps and numerous cairns marking the site of former extensive quarrying operations that extracted gritstone

Fossdale seen from the cairns on the lower slopes of Stags Fell

across a pasture to another gate, then to the top edge of a little plantation where it turns south and downhill again. Reaching a gate at the walled Shutt Lane, turn downhill and follow it into and through the quiet and attractive village of Sedbusk. Bear left at the junction just beyond the Primitive Methodist Chapel and then curve right on a downhill bend.

Almost immediately you will see a finger-post on the right, signed for Haylands Bridge.

The path crosses two fields by slit-stiles, crosses the Hardraw-Askrigg road and continues across more fields to regain the road just north of Haylands Bridge. From here the outward route is reversed back to the car park.

143

31.   The Swale Gorge and Swinner Gill

Best map: OS 1:25,000 Yorkshire Dales (Northern
    & Central Areas)

Distance: About 9 miles/14.4km

Highest elevation reached: 1411ft/430m

Height gained: 492ft/150m approx.

Overall star rating: ***

General level of exertion needed: Medium

Time for the round: About 4–5 hours

Terrain: Almost all on good paths in this
    limestone area with a splendid (optional) gill
    scramble.

Swaledale is haunted by the ghosts of the lead-mining industry that developed here from Roman times to a last great surge in the nineteenth century, when about four thousand men were employed, and the slowly healing scars left on the landscape are still visible, particularly on the moors and gills on the northern side of the dale. This walk combines superb landscape with a few glimpses into that remarkable past.

Parking isn't easy in Thwaite (grid ref. 892982) but you'll manage somewhere. Then, to get started, find Kearton's well known guest house-cum-shop, turn right in front of it and find a Pennine Way sign in a corner, just to the right of a five-barred farm gate. The path now leads across fields, then slants across the slopes of the hill of Kisdon straight ahead, with good views back to Thwaite, the Butter Tubs road and Great Shunner Fell. Just beyond Kisdon Farm, cross the old corpse road from Keld to Muker and follow Pennine Way signs contouring round the eastern flank of the hill along an alternately green and rocky path. For a long way, you look right into the dark, scarred hollows of Swinner Gill on the other side of the valley, then the gorge becomes much more wooded and water can be heard thundering in the depths below a great white limestone cliff where the river bends. Then across a dip, there's a glimpse ahead of the scattered houses at Keld.

Just before the dip, there's a finger-post for Muker, slanting down into the lower gorge. It is well worth following it for a few yards until a steep path leads off left down through trees to limestone shelves on this side of the River Swale for a fine view of the splendid lower and upper falls of Kisdon Force. Return to the upper path leading almost into the quiet village; ignore the sign to the upper falls, since that is an awkward way of getting to the lower ones, which are

The gorge of Swinner Gill

145

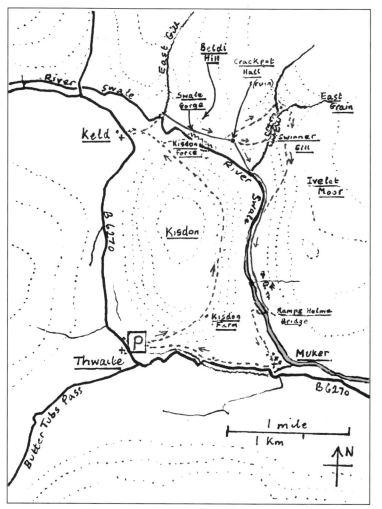

better. Instead, take the Pennine Way lane off to the right, down to a footbridge and a delightful junction where East Gill beck joins the main river with a little cascade.

Leave the Pennine Way here, turn right over the bridge and up the broad track heading towards the Swale gorge, with the tree-filled depths below and the steep slopes of Beldi Hill above on the left. Shortly the track kinks to the left, where a path leads up into the combe above and to the old Beldi Mine lead-workings, but the main track leads to a fork just beyond a barn. Take the right fork to the crumbling ruins of Crackpot Hall which, in the 1760s, was at the centre of a great legal (and at times physical) battle between the rival Beldi Hill Company and the Wharton Estate whose miners were in Swinner Gill. The Hall was finally abandoned about 1950 but it commands marvellous views over the valley of the Swale.

There's now a choice of three ways. Either return to the main track which descends to the valley bottom. Or, much better, go well above Crackpot Hall by a high-level path traversing round into the upper part of Swinner Gill. Thirdly, for a grand little adventure, descend very slightly from the ruin, round the hillside on a narrow path leading to the bottom of the narrow and steep gorge in Swinner Gill. Particularly if there's a good flow of water you can now have a splendid scramble up the gill on ledges, squeezing round and over huge water-worn boulders. If you're just a big kid like me, you'll love it: after Hell Gill, it's the best scramble I can think of in the Dales. You emerge at a junction of two gills above the gorge with a waterfall in the right-hand one, a mine tunnel right next to it and the ruins of old mine buildings just above; you would have reached the same point by the higher traverse-line from the Hall, but without the fun.

After a look round here, you can reverse the scramble to retreat, or take a slanting path contouring out of the gill at the level of the waterfall, passing above the gorge and following a natural ledge for a way; then you descend on a reasonable path to the good track in the valley bottom and so to the Ramps Holme (foot)bridge over the Swale. You will reach the bridge by the other routes mentioned also.

Signs lead now to Muker, and more to Thwaite via Usha Gap Farm where you join the road briefly before more signs and stiles lead pleasantly back to Thwaite. However, don't try doing the last bit, as I once did, in the dark and in pouring rain. Even with a head-torch I lost the way and, with my two dogs, took over an hour for a fifteen-minute journey, climbing what felt like twenty walls on the way.

Kisdon Force

147

32.   Gunnerside Gill and the Lead Mines

Best map: OS 1:25,000 Yorkshire Dales (Northern & Central areas)

Distance: About 11 miles/17.7km or 10 miles/16.1km for the easier walk

Highest elevation reached: 2205ft/672m (or 1903ft/580m for the shorter walk)

Height gained: 1450ft/442m (or 1122ft/342m for the easier walk)

Overall star rating: **

General level of exertion needed: Medium/high

Time for the round: About 6½–7 hours (or 5½–6 hours for the shorter version)

Terrain: On good paths – except for the approach to Rogan's Seat.

This is a fine walk, of very varied landscape and with much of absorbing interest. Gunnerside Gill, at the heart of a lead-mining industry, which reached a climax about a century ago and employed as many as four thousand miners, has much more to show than industrial dereliction. I am personally surprised at how few visible remains there are.

Park in Gunnerside, where there is a little car park by the bridge (grid ref. 983951), then take the path up the east side of the pleasantly wooded gill, soon climbing gently to the top edge of the trees. After a while, the path descends to the gill again, by a barn, where it is broad and open. On the right of the stream and beside the path are some ruined buildings and a line of 'bings' or bunkers, which were used for holding ore. Ahead, the path leads away from the bed of the gill over a stile through the wall, and it is advisable to use it for it leads to a very pleasant broad and grassy track.

Before crossing the stile, however, more ruins and spoil-heaps are to be seen on the other side of the stream, with what looks like a rusty old boiler lying on its side on the bank. This was the compressed-air tank at the Sir Francis Mine, the last major enterprise of the industry and a remarkable one, when a level was driven into the lower limestones as the upper ones were being exhausted of ore. Work began in 1864 but after five years' progress was reduced to 10 feet per month and Sir George Denys Bt introduced a McKean borer, driven by compressed air, the power for which came from a 39-ft diameter water-wheel. The new technique enabled the ore in the Friarfold Vein to be reached seven years later, in 1877. By 1880, it was said that a man could go underground in

Gunnerside Gill in winter with the ruins of the Bunton Mine buildings

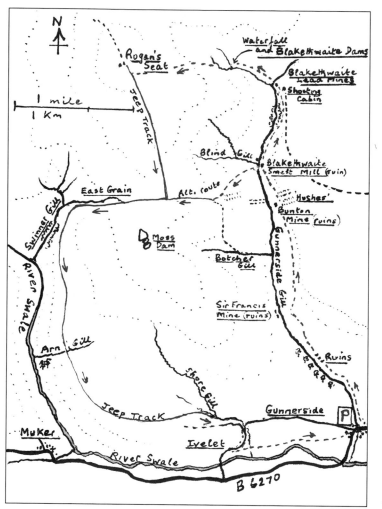

Gunnerside Gill and emerge into daylight in Arkengarthdale six miles away but by then the industry was on its last legs as lead prices plummeted.

Continue up the green track, past Botcher Gill, to reach more bunkers and the ruins of the Bunton Mine buildings. Paths now pick ways across three great shallow gullies or 'hushes' – Bunton, Friarfold and Gorton – where earlier ore-seeking methods involved making a dam on top of the moor, then breaking it suddenly to send a rush of water scouring the fellside and revealing the ore veins. It doesn't matter which path you take, though the lower one leads directly to the junction where Blind Gill joins Gunnerside Gill. Here, across a single stone-slab bridge, are the remains of the Blakethwaite Smelt Mill (not named on the OS map) where sulphur was burnt out of the ore and it became malleable and formed into 'pigs'; on this side of the stream can be seen the four arches of the building where peat was stored to dry out. On the hillside above is a limekiln, used for making mortar.

Keep on a little further up the main gill, on either side of the stream, to one more ruin near a flat area, beyond which the gill narrows through a limestone gorge. Ahead is a last small ruin and sheepfold beside the stream and above, at a higher level, a solid shooting-hut beside a track that leads immediately to the disused Blakethwaite Lead Mines. Keep on to reach a waterfall and immediately above it the remains of the Blakethwaite Dams which were used to build up a head of water for the water-wheels at the smelt-mill lower down.

Beyond, lie acres of rolling, heather-covered moor and due west, a mile away across them, lies the top of Rogan's Seat. There's your summit, after a struggle across deep heather and even deeper groughs in the peat. (If you can't face it, retreat down to Blind Gill and a track will be found leading west over to Swinner Gill anyway.) If you accept the challenge, it will be a relief to reach a wire fence beside a good jeep track and totter up to the cairn on top of a peat hag which marks the summit. After the moor, the jeep tracks will be irresistible, winding south with the glint of water on Moss Dam ahead. Turn west at the junction with the track from Blind Gill and follow it to where it starts to descend East Grain to Swinner Gill. Here a footpath sign shows a way down to Swinner Gill, worth descending if you've not been down there before (*see* Walk 31), but otherwise stay with the main track, keeping just outside the intake wall, above Arn Gill and Ivelet Side, with easy walking on the highest level above the Swale valley and leading nicely to the tarmac beside Shore Gill and just above Gunnerside Lodge.

Turn downhill here to Ivelet village, and a signed way will be found beside the telephone box leading over a footbridge and giving a delightful ramble over the fields back to Gunnerside.

Gunnerside Gill: the compression tank for the Sir Francis Mine

151

To Great Whernside from Old Cote Moor

PART FOUR

Wharfedale, Littondale and Nidderdale

33. Malham Cove and Gordale Scar

Best map: OS 1:25,000 Yorkshire Dales (Southern area)

Distance: About 4½ miles/7.2km or 6 miles/9.6km for the longer walk

Highest elevation reached: 1247ft/380m

Height gained: 558ft/170m

Overall star rating: ***

General level of exertion required: Low/medium

Time for the round: About 3 hours or 4 hours for the longer walk; neither should be rushed

Terrain: All on good paths except when scrambling up Gordale Scar, which is optional on the shorter walk described.

It doesn't matter how many times you go: Malham Cove and Gordale Scar are terrific, impressive, set amidst all those fields and walls. Both places are understandably popular, so if you seek tranquillity, go mid-week. There is a mass of paths around this area and it's a problem to decide how to link all the best scenic bits without going over some of the ground twice, so the first description is of a shorter walk linking Malham Cove, Gordale Scar and the pretty waterfall of Janet's Foss, in a clockwise direction from Malham; a suggestion for a longer version follows.

As you approach Malham, the great sweep of the Cove is visible from some way off and becomes an irresistible first objective if you've never been before. The car park, which is well signed, is at grid ref. 900627. Walk north up the road for a little way to an obvious stile and path (also part of the Pennine Way path) heading across the sloping pastures towards the Cove itself. What a tremendous wall, and it is, of course, a climbers' playground. I'll never forget trying to get over that great overhanging roof, seen as you look up to the right of the centre of the Cove; I put all my weight on to an old iron peg which suddenly tilted downwards – and I nearly fell off with fright! Nor will I forget abseiling down Main Wall (the one to the left of the overhang) in the dark and discovering rather too late that the ropes didn't reach the bottom so I had to drop off into the river. On a recent visit we watched in astonishment as three divers emerged from the water flowing from the base of the great cliff; they had just penetrated about three hundred yards, following the water back under the rock.

Walking up the stepped track to the left of the Cove quickly leads to a tremendous viewpoint, the marvellous pavement of clints and grikes running

Malham Cove, seen from the clints on top

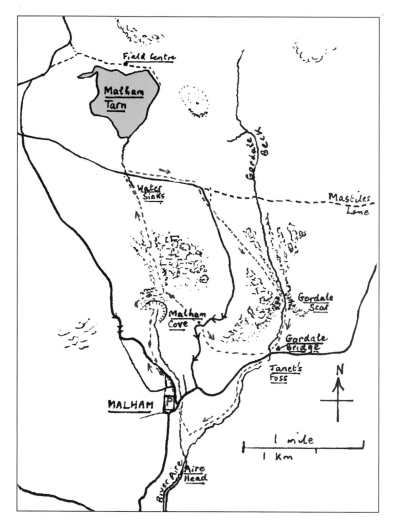

along the top. A dry valley runs back inland from the edge where once a waterfall poured over the lip in a colossal cascade about three hundred feet high. From the dry river bed, a stile leads south-east over the wall, signed for Gordale, and a delightful grassy path climbs up the field, then descends to cross the tarmac road of Malham Rakes, and continues in a curving line round the pastures, with fine views of the mosaic of ancient walls to the east of Gordale House. It descends to reach the road again at Gordale Bridge where the obvious track leads directly towards the great jaws of Gordale Scar. This is in some ways even more impressive than Malham Cove for you have the sense of being almost enclosed in a vast cavern where the sky is just a slit of blue, and an upper waterfall pours out of a hole high in the cliff-face above. Most reasonably active walkers will want to penetrate to the upper part of the gorge which is easy enough by means of a little scramble up a pock-marked tongue of rock sticking through the lower waterfall on its left side; here you join a path beyond leading up and out of the gorge.

Retrace your steps to the road, walk along it south-westwards towards Malham but in just a few yards take the path off to the left, obvious and well-signed, to Janet's Foss. This lovely waterfall is quickly reached, then the path winds through the wood, emerges onto pasture and, well-signed, reaches Malham again at some stepping-stones over the stream.

* *

For a longer walk, I enjoy starting as in the shorter version described above but then going north-west from the top of Malham Cove up the dry valley, fringed with little cliffs and scars, following the course of the original river. When it swings sharply right at a steep cliff, the path kinks with it (sign for 'Water Sinks'). It is rocky for a way, then becomes a green path to Water Sinks where the stream flowing from Malham Tarn disappears into the ground, re-appearing not at the foot of Malham Cove, as you might expect, but at Aire Head, where the River Aire rises, further south. Malham Tarn is not visible yet but the path leads on and it soon comes into sight, lying on a bed of impervious Silurian slates and boulder clay amidst surrounding porous limestone rocks.

Turn right (east) on reaching the tarmac road. It is unfenced so you can walk on grass beside it for about half a mile until the road swings south-east. Continue just a little further beside the tarmac and then go through a slit-stile on the left where there is a sign for Gordale; this is reached along a green sward between limestone pavements and has a descent into the top end of Gordale Scar, giving perhaps an even more dramatic approach than from below. Return by way of Janet's Foss as described above.

Looking down Gordale Scar

34. Posforth Gill and Simon's Seat

Best map: OS 1:25,000 Yorkshire Dales (Southern area)

Distance: About 8 miles/12.8km

Highest elevation reached: 1591ft/485m

Height gained: 1086ft/331m

Overall star rating: **

General level of exertion needed: Medium

Time for the round: About 4 hours

Terrain: All on paths, although the high moor can be wet and muddy.

Although this very interesting short day includes a two-mile stretch across the top of the private grouse moor of Barden Fell which can really only be described as boring, the rest of the walk can be enchanting. I say 'can be' because Wharfedale near Bolton Abbey may at times seem like a Dales version of Blackpool beach. So if you want to avoid crowds, go early or go out of season. *Please note: no dogs allowed.*

If you simply want to climb to the fine viewpoint and most dramatic crags of Simon's Seat, it can be done in a 3½ mile/5.6km version by parking at Howgill (grid ref. 065592). Then follow Howgill Lane to a gate onto the fellside just before Dalehead Farm, from where a steep path snakes up through bracken and then heather directly to the top.

For the full round, it is probably best to park at Bolton Abbey's Riverside (or Pavilion) car park (fee) at grid ref. 078552, although canny people can park a few cars for nothing on the other side of the River Wharfe at grid ref. 078557, where the walk starts anyway.

Assuming you start from the Riverside car park, cross the Wharfe by the wooden bridge opposite, walk left up the road for two hundred yards (past the canny parking spot) and through a gate on the right by Waterfall Cottage where there is one of the Devonshire Estate's access signs. The path now leads over pasture on the right of the woods of Posforth Gill and through what should, in a half century or so's time, be a fine avenue of a hundred oaks planted in 1980 to commemorate the Golden Jubilee of the West Riding Area of the Ramblers' Association. At the end of the avenue, veer left on the lower path, leading quickly to the fine twin spouts of Posforth Force pouring over an edge of gritstone boulders into a shallow pool. The upper path (which you didn't take and which leads above the Force) has been diverted by a landslide so

Simon's Seat

159

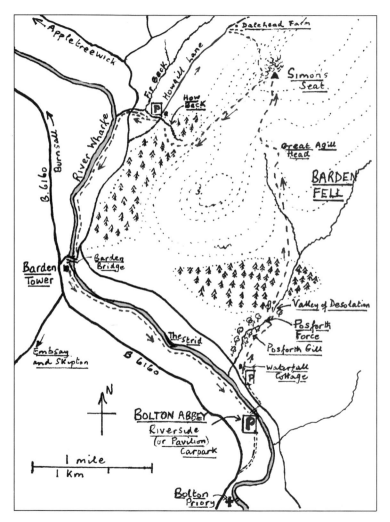

it's now easier and more interesting to hop across the beck on the large boulders and go up the opposite bank on a path which quickly passes a footbridge and leads into the oddly-named Valley of Desolation. This is a thickly wooded and delightful little valley whose trees were once flattened in a big storm over a century ago, hence the name.

A quarter of a mile above Posforth Force are some more cascades, widely-spaced twin falls, but the path is signed off left before reaching these (you can't get beyond them without problems anyway) and slants up to a stile, through a conifer plantation and on to open moor. The dull section follows: a steady slog takes you up the side of Great Agill Beck, until gritstone tors begin to appear dotted amongst the heather and the well-cairned path leads remorselessly to the highest, Simon's Seat. When I came up this way with my young son and his friend aged ten, the friend asked me what these piles of stones (cairns) were. To his (temporary) great consternation I told him that the corpses of walkers who just couldn't make it to the top were buried under them.

The rocks are about sixty feet high on the northern flank and stand proudly on the edge of the moor, giving an extensive view; some people think it is the finest view of all up Wharfedale, although I personally think that the view from Conistone Pie (see Walk 37) is better. The tors make a good spot to stop for a while before striking off to the south-west on a peaty track signed for Howgill. This soon descends towards the valley down the edge of How Beck, crosses Howgill

Lane and completes the descent to the Appletreewick road at a footbridge over Fir Beck. From here a signed path – which is now the Dales Way – leads easily towards the Wharfe again and is followed along the river bank to the much loved Barden Bridge.

A diversion over the bridge and up the road on the other side to the romantic ruins of Barden Tower (and the former chapel now farmhouse next to it selling teas) may well appeal, after which you return to the river bank and make a choice as to which side to take for the final stretch. The west bank forms part of a Nature Trail passing The Strid – the famous narrowing of the river in its limestone bed, where legend and history as to who met his death trying to leap it while chasing deer seem to have got inextricably mingled – but it's the better path and allows a pleasant and straightforward return to the Riverside car park.

Posforth Force

161

35. The Western Skyline of Barden Moor

Best map: OS 1:25,000 Yorkshire Dales (Southern area)

Distance: About 11 miles/17.6km for the round; 7½ miles/12km for the traverse

Highest elevation reached: 1640ft/500m

Height gained: 984ft/300m

Overall star rating: */**

General level of exertion needed: Medium/high

Time: About 6 hours for the round; about 4 hours for the traverse

Terrain: Mostly on rough gritstone moorland paths, fairly wet at times.

Barden Moor is a heather-clad private grouse moor to the west of the River Wharfe. It is closed, although never on a Sunday, for thirty days during the shooting season following the 'glorious twelfth' of August, and details of these days, and the other reasonable restrictions, are posted at the various entry points to the moor. Incidentally, there is now much evidence that the management of these and other moors for grouse is a major factor in retaining the heather, which would otherwise yield to bracken, a plant of no value whatsoever; the heather also provides cover for many species of moorland birds. Walkers used to the freedom of other fells may feel less irked by the restrictions when they appreciate this – rather than just being told 'Keep out'.

The highlight of this walk is undoubtedly the splendid tramp along the line of gritstone edges which mark the western edge of the moor. Short expeditions from Rylstone or Cracoe up to the moor's edge and down again are feasible, but the dramatic skyline which is well seen above the Skipton to Grassington road is far too good to be chopped up into little sections. I therefore propose two possibilities: one a circuit, returning to the start; the other a traverse, for which you will either need two cars or an obliging driver to drop you and collect you later.

Let's take the traverse first. The start of the walk is at Embsay Moor Reservoir (grid ref. 998544): you can't park there but you can be dropped off. Reach it by driving from Skipton to Embsay village and then for a mile up Pasture Road opposite the post office. Walkers now take the bridleway signed around the water and then climb up to the fine height of Embsay Crag. From here you can descend a little towards the reservoir before climbing up again to Crookrise Crag but I prefer to strike across to the fine gritstone

Gritstone outcrop, Deer Gallows Ridge, Embsay Moor

163

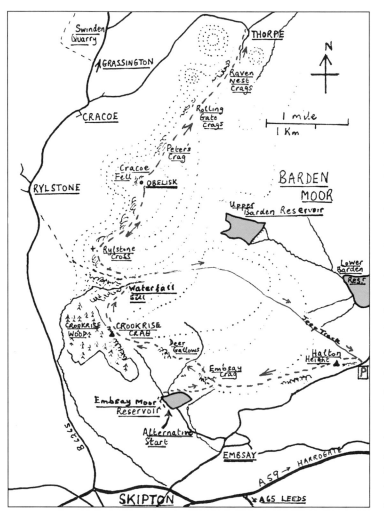

outcrop of Deer Gallows Ridge, reached by contouring rather than descending, and then continuing along the contour to the edge of Crookrise Crag which rises above the wood. Keep along the edge but then, as Waterfall Gill comes in sight, strike inland to cross it, thus not losing too much height. You will shortly afterwards cross the path which runs from Rylstone to Halton Heights, and Rylstone Cross will be visible ahead as the next objective; this is in an airy position on a gritstone edge overlooking the vale below which runs from Flasby to Cracoe.

Yet further along the moor's edge is the Cracoe War Memorial, a striking obelisk visible for many miles and soon reached, with views northwards to Grassington and Wharfedale. Still the edge leads on: Peter's Crag, Bartle Crag, Rolling Gate Crags and, finally, although the sharp edge is fading away now and you need to descend a little, to Raven Nest Crags. Here you are above a group of very green, distinctively rounded limestone hills which are below the general level of the moor. They are called reef knolls and are apparently believed to have been formed rather like the Great Barrier Reef off the coast of Queensland in Australia, from the fossilised sea creatures that once inhabited a warm sea lapping at the edge of higher land. It is a thought to make one realise the immensity of past time, the shortness of our own mortality – and the monstrosity of Swinden Quarry on the other side of the Grassington road which chews away at one of these hillocks in order to obtain limestone needed to build more motorways which will choke up more and more of our congested little island. Another sermon over.

The intake wall is very near now, and the walled lane down to Thorpe village. I hope your transport is there too so that you can retreat from a fine outing and continue philosophising in a comfortable pub on the way home.

For the circuit, or round, I suggest you drive to the highest point of the road with access to the moor near Halton Height (grid ref. 037554), and leave the car there. Don't set off on the track signed for Rylstone on the edge of the moor (the old medieval road to Bolton Abbey and which is used for the return) but go due west towards a compact group of gritstone rocks and then towards a single rock on the skyline. The trig point of Halton Height (1171ft/357m) above High Crag is just beyond this and you are now on course. Skirt the wood ahead and then follow the sketchy path alongside the boundary wall and then up to the high land of Embsay Crag, a clearly seen objective ahead and the first of a series of fine viewpoints. Continue, as already described above for the traverse as far as the obelisk, the war memorial above Cracoe which should not be missed, then return to Rylstone Cross. Heading south-east from here and just north of Waterfall Gill, you will quickly reach the line of the old track from Cracoe, although here it's not much more than a sketchy path marked by an occasional post in the boggy ground. This, however, very quickly becomes a good track, used on

Embsay Moor Reservoir

shooting days, with occasional stone culverts for drainage. It leads very easily and pleasantly eastwards to the top of the moor and just as gently down the other slope back to the car.

36.   The Wharfe and Trollers Gill

Best map: OS 1:25,000 Yorkshire Dales (Southern area)

Distance: About 7½miles/12km

Highest elevation reached: 984ft/300m

Height gained: 459ft/140m

Overall star rating: * *

General level of exertion needed: Low/medium

Time for the round: About 3½–4 hours

Terrain: Nearly all on good paths and tracks. Troller's Gill is rougher and there is about half a mile of tarmac.

The section of the River Wharfe from Burnsall to Howgill (part of the Dales Way) is particularly beautiful, while Trollers Gill is a real surprise, quite delightful and definitely not to be by-passed: another hidden Dales gem. The bit of tarmac that links the two halves of this walk is soon forgotten.

Burnsall is a most attractive village, one of the oldest in Wharfedale and much loved for its open village green and picnic places near the river bridge. Park in the car park at grid ref. 032611, then cross the bridge to the eastern bank and go through the slot in the wall on the other side where a finger-post points the way to Howgill across a loop in the river. You will see the round shape of Kail Hill ahead and the more distant rise of Barden Fell on the skyline.

The way ahead is well marked, running close to the bank after passing Woodhouse Farm, then by-passing Appletreewick. The riverside views become particularly fine as the Wharfe is forced to swing east and enters a narrow, wooded gorge with rapids and swirling pools. Emerging from the ravine, the path veers away left towards the hamlet of Howgill, reaching a road where a bridge crosses Fir Beck.

Ignore the sign 'FP Howgill Lane' opposite (which would take you below Barden Fell and Simon's Seat) and instead turn left up the tarmac road for just a few paces to find a stile on the right signed 'Public Footpath Skyreholme'. This path crosses pasture a little way back from and above the left bank of Fir Beck and passes a nicely concealed caravan site in a dell beside the beck to reach Howarth Farm and the tarmac road. Here you turn right (north-east) and press on to a T-junction and a sign for the attractive house and grounds of Parcevall Hall. Go towards the hall but leave the tarmac just before reaching the bridge across the stream at the entrance to the grounds where there's a gate on the left and a

The River Wharfe near Appletreewick

167

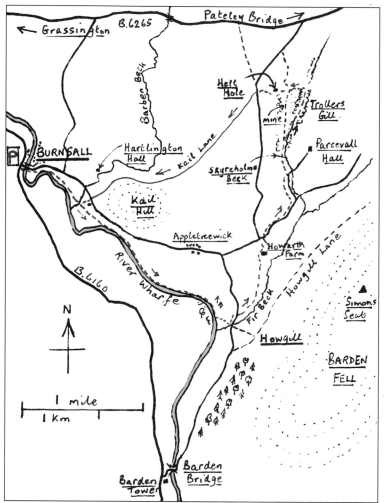

currently very faded sign for 'Gill Heads and New Road'.

A pleasant path now leads up a steep-sided, pretty, wooded valley, then into a once-dammed broad and grassy basin, but with limestone walls rising steeply ahead. The valley forks and the signed footpath takes the left branch (leading up to and beyond the workings of Gill Head Mine) and consequently misses out what I think is the most interesting part of this half of the walk. So take the right-hand branch instead, which turns a corner and leads to a rocky path up the mostly dry bed of the splendid Trollers Gill which, with its overhanging limestone walls, is rather like a miniature Gordale Scar. Rock-climbers are frequent visitors here as can be seen from the occasional bit of nylon tape dangling from the crags. As the steep walls fade away into the moor, the stream appears above ground again and although the gill continues a little further, the best is over and there is a way out up the left bank to a stile and over the little rise beyond, to reach the mine road. Those who had taken the left fork lower down would join again here.

Turn right here, follow the track round a left-hand bend and then, as it swings right again, leave it for a faint path leading west across the moor; this passes the gurgling pothole of Hell Hole just as you leave the main track. A short walk across open moor leads to a stile onto the road going back to Skyreholme. Turn left (south) along this and then in a hundred paces or so take the track on the right signed for Hartlington. It is now a straightforward return, for this track goes

Trollers Gill

first over open pasture and then, as Kail Hill comes into view again, leads all the way down the old walled track of Kail Lane, with a pleasing view of Hartlington Hall on the other bank of the Barben Beck. The track reaches the Burnsall to Appletreewick road just near Woodhouse Farm again. Cross the road to rejoin the Dales Way path along the river and you will reach Burnsall in about fifteen minutes.

37. Grassington's Old Lead Mines

Best map: OS 1:25,000 Yorkshire Dales (Southern area)

Distance: About 4 miles/6.4km

Highest elevation reached: 1247ft/380m

Height gained: 535ft/163m

Overall star rating: *

General level of exertion needed: Low

Time for the round: About 2½–3 hours

Terrain: Mostly on good paths up the gill and on the moor; faint paths across grass on the return. Not too many stiles.

Until you've actually been to and seen the place with your own eyes, it is difficult to grasp the fact that this high, bleak, open moor, the natural home of grouse and curlew, was once an industrial landscape of great complexity, where lead was mined in vast quantity for two centuries or so. This short walk leads up an attractive gill with a fascinating glimpse of the extraordinary life that must have been led when there were moving wire-ropes running over pulleys and across the moor, waterwheels driving pumps and crushing machines, furnaces roaring away and a great chimney high up on the moor belching smoke.

Find a parking spot in Hebden village (grid ref. 025632) near the school or just up the tarmac lane beside Hebden Beck on the north side of the main road. You may find a none too obvious little path up the east bank of the beck but it is simpler to walk up the tarmac lane on the west bank to begin with. After a second gate, the gill looks accessible by way of a field-gate on the right, which leads to an attractive view of Scale Force in the wooded ravine, but you need to retreat, pass the cottage named 'Jerry and Ben's' and continue a few more yards up the road to the cottages at Hole Bottom. Take the right fork here which does lead up the gill, an unmade track winding up this attractive valley fringed with gritstone crags. Time is now softening the scars of the past, a century after the last great surge of lead extraction ceased, but just beyond the second gate across the track can be seen the blocked-off portal that is the end of the Duke's Level; this was a tunnel that took over twenty years to build in the 1820s and drained the whole of the Grassington ore-field of the water seeping into mine-shafts which were by then as much as 400 feet deep. A little further on are some derelict ruins, then on the right is the end of Bolton Gill with more spoil-heaps.

Looking up Hebden Gill from near Hole Bottom

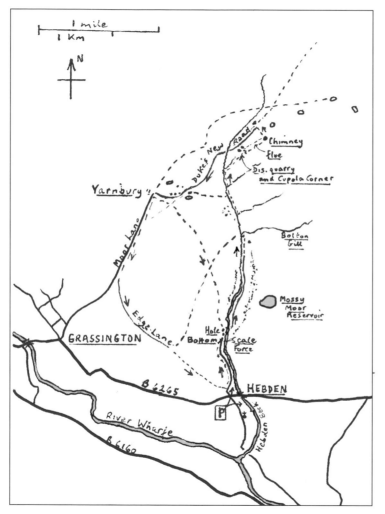

The good track ends, you cross the stream easily and follow a lesser path up the left bank to more extensive spoil-heaps. From here you can get first sight of the chimney over to the north-east with some odd-looking ruins to its left. My own first sight of that chimney in such an unexpected place quickened my interest enormously and I rushed up the rest of the gill as fast as I could go, completely intrigued. I clambered up a side-stream to get nearer, then over a stile into the fenced-off area where there is a large notice-board defining the various parts and warning where there is a risk of subsidence. I didn't need to be told what I could see when I climbed out of a former quarry and found I was next to an enormously long flue tunnelled across the moor. It was collapsing in places to reveal its construction, and heading straight for the chimney. The roar up that chimney must have really been something! And the poor devils who had to clean it out often had to do so while it was still hot.

The ruins near the chimney were apparently the site of the crushing mill and happily, for an uninstructed visit as my own first one was, there are boards here too explaining the various processes. With a little imagination you can get a very good idea of what a tremendous industry there was here but much damage was done when the area was used as a gunnery range during the Second World War and what was left was adapted by a chemical company in the 1950s who extracted fluorspar from the spoil-heaps. Walking south-westwards from the chimney leads one along the Duke's New Road to the buildings at Yarnbury.

You pass more old tips, a little reservoir and a line of what look like old craters but are in fact collapsed bell-pits. Here miners dug a shaft down into the ground, chasing the vein of ore and enlarging the bottom of the shaft as far as they dared.

To get back to Hebden, there's a finger-post pointing virtually due south to a footpath across pastures but most of the stiles on the way are just slits in the wall and not too easy to spot. If you lose the path as I have done, you'll have to trend left back towards Hebden Beck, so getting back to Hole Bottom again. Or, with more certainty, follow the grassy edge of Moor Lane back towards Grassington and then the old track of Edge Lane and more obvious paths south-eastwards back to the village.

Left: *The smelt mill flue and chimney near Grassington*

Above: *Collapsed bell pits on Grassington Moor*

38.   Grassington to Kettlewell

<table>
<tr><td>Best map: OS 1:25,000 Yorkshire Dales (Southern area)</td></tr>
<tr><td>Distance: About 6½ miles/10.4km</td></tr>
<tr><td>Highest elevation reached: 1083ft/330m</td></tr>
<tr><td>Height gained: 459ft/140m</td></tr>
<tr><td>Overall star rating: ***</td></tr>
<tr><td>General level of exertion needed: Low/medium</td></tr>
<tr><td>Time for the walk: About 3 hours</td></tr>
<tr><td>Terrain: Almost all on grassy paths; quite a few stiles.</td></tr>
</table>

This is a superb walk along limestone shelves above the valley of the River Wharfe, one of the finest in the Dales on a good day and should be on every moderate walker's list. I should mention that the alternative final bit of the walk as I describe it, using a track beside Dowber Gill to descend to Kettlewell, is just off the 'best map' but you'll find it on the 1:25,000 Yorkshire Dales (Northern & Central areas) map. The walk can't really be turned into a round and a satisfactory return needs transport. Possibilities include: having a willing driver who will collect you at the end of the walk; having two cars and leaving one in Kettlewell (or two cars and two groups of walkers swapping keys half way); check in Grassington to see if there's a suitable bus from Kettlewell (unlikely); or, as I did recently, putting a push-bike in the car boot and taking it to Kettlewell to use for the return to Grassington.

Whichever you choose, the Information Centre and car park in Grassington is on the Pateley Bridge road at grid ref. 002637. From here, turn left and then into the cobbled square and a walk north-eastwards up the main village street (the road leading to Yarnbury), past many tempting coffee shops, quickly leads to a crossroads and a left turn into Chapel Street. When this swings sharp left downhill at Town Head, turn in to the farm on the right and curve left between two large buildings to find a sign for Conistone as you leave the yard. Just beyond, go through the middle of three gates, then cross the field to pass through a tight slot in the wall.

Now follow the green way curving across more pasture towards the top end of Grass Wood and, using two more stiles close together, go into the huge open field called Lea Green, with a little limestone escarpment on the left. This is the site of a mediaeval settlement whose field system is apparently best seen from the air and no doubt the line of the Dales Way is

Looking up Wharfedale to Knipe Scar from Conistone Pie

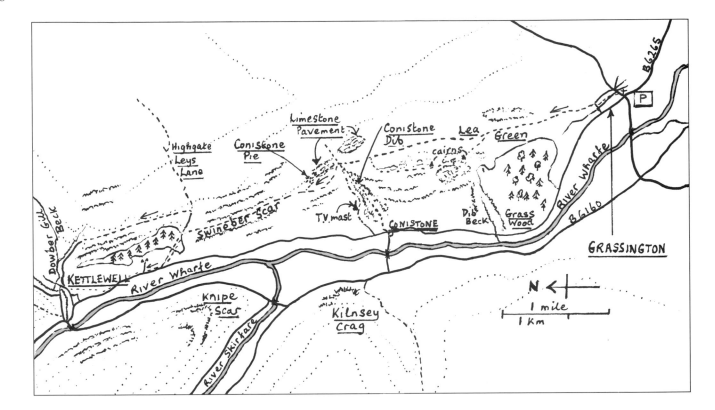

best seen from up there too; it is not very clear on the ground as it is confused by other tracks. However, heading north up the field and over the rise reveals a fine limestone pavement on the far slope of a valley. This valley contains Dib Beck and there are two prominent cairns on the skyline beyond it.

Having got this far, it will become clear that the official path is going to bend round the head of this valley to the east, where a ladder-stile is now visible, and the path does in fact then run along a shallow trench with the clints on the left hand and green fields on the right. My own exploratory urge is sometimes too strong to just stick with the official line and on one occasion I crossed to the splendid clint field where the wall was low and then climbed to the cairns. Beyond, a line of limestone edges lead northwards and the walls all abut against the crags so that it is easy to climb a bit of crag and the walls at the same time. The OS map shows more ancient settlements along here and for a moment I thought I'd found another 'Celtic Wall' like the one below Smearsett Scar in Craven. It wasn't though and when I saw the radio mast ahead and Kilnsey Crag across the valley floor, I decided it was as well to curtail my diversion and rejoin the official way by veering back right to reach the head of the splendid little dry valley of Conistone Dib.

On the other side, a four-way finger-post, just beyond the jeep track running down to Conistone, points the Dales Way walker along a green track, but it runs just below a magnificent limestone pavement that should not be missed. This has a fine example of a lime-kiln on its eastern edge and the pavement comes to an end just before reaching the unmistakable little natural limestone eminence of Conistone Pie, with a square funnel sticking up above its crust. This is a splendid vantage for the view up Wharfedale ahead, with Knipe Scar like the prow of a great ship separating the waters of the River Skirfare in Littondale from those of the Wharfe.

The way ahead is very clear now, with a line of stiles along the top of Swineber Scar until it meets the conifer wood where Highgate Leys Lane rises from the

Conistone Pie

valley. The official way descends to the road from here and is then signed into Kettlewell but I don't like walking on tarmac and can recommend turning right (south-east) up the track of Highgate Leys Lane until you are just above the level of the wood and can then turn north onto another grassy path along more fine limestone shelves. I've never found the 'settlements and field systems' shown on the OS map along here but this delightful path soon joins a good track just above Dowber Gill which then winds down into Kettlewell.

177

39. The Monk's Road

Best map: OS 1:25,000 Yorkshire Dales (Southern area)

Distance: About 9½ miles/15.2km

Highest elevation reached: 1640ft/500m

Height gained: 1148ft/350m

Overall star rating: *

General level of exertion needed: Medium

Time for the round: About 4½–5 hours

Terrain: On reasonable paths and tracks over limestone pasture – and therefore dry underfoot – for most of the way.

This is essentially a simple two-way crossing, with some good views, of the mass of high limestone country to the north-east of Malham Tarn. You make use of an ancient path, the Monk's Road, which was probably used by the monks when Fountains Fell was sheep pasture for Fountains Abbey.

Arncliffe is a lovely village in Littondale, with an ancient and delightfully-situated church beside the River Skirfare. It has a fine green with an old pump, attractive cottages and a good pub, The Falcon.

There is usually room to park nearby (grid ref. 932718) and the walk starts from beside it, up the walled lane signed 'Malham'. It appears to be heading for the steep defile of Cow Close Beck which is funnelled between steep grass slopes on the one hand and sharp limestone scars on the other but the lane can soon be seen to end at a field gate only a short distance ahead. The path (the 'road') takes the stile on the right and climbs up the field to a grassy way on the first limestone ledge. It then proceeds via more stiles to a second ledge running along the top of Yew Cogar Scar, with Cowside Beck flowing along the open-sided ravine below and with splendid views up Littondale. Shortly, however, the path veers away from the line of the gill below, climbs gently to higher land, becoming less defined on the rockier ground, but always heading south-east below the highest scars on the skyline. Passing to the left of a little tarn, the path curves more to the south below a line of scars, while ahead can be seen the first clump of trees since leaving Arncliffe. Just before reaching them a finger-post is passed, signed 'B. W. Arncliffe 3, F.P. Darn-brook 1½' where a footpath heads off to the north-west towards Darnbrook Beck (see Walk 14, Fountains Fell). The path continues onward to skirt the buildings of Middle House sheltering beneath the trees, which themselves must have been protected as

Arncliffe and Cowside Beck from Old Cote Moor; the Monk's Road goes left above Arncliffe

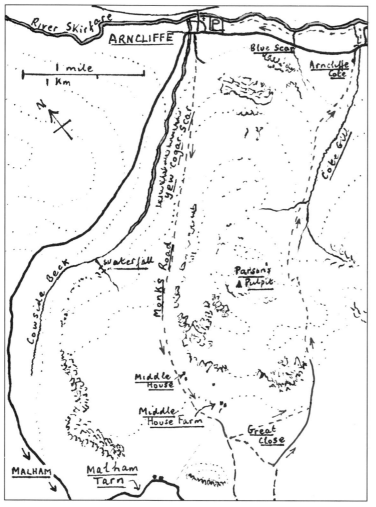

saplings since the natural ones don't stand a chance against the sheep. Middle House may have been a grange for Middle House Farm, a little further on; it was clearly neglected for many a long year but now seems to be in the process of some sort of restoration.

To the right of Middle House, the path briefly joins then leaves a track to reach a stile, and beyond that and at a lower level is another stile and path, still heading south-east and skirting Middle House Farm itself. On the descent, you get a brief glimpse of Malham Tarn behind a broad, flattish plain with Great Close Hill in its middle. In several places little streams well up out of the ground, showing where the waters draining from the surrounding limestone have reached the beds of slates and clays on which the tarn lies. Not surprisingly, the lush plain of Great Close was a former fattening-up ground for Scottish cattle on their way through the Dales to English markets.

The line of the Monks Road, which shadows the telegraph posts over the col towards Malham Tarn, is left here near Middle House Farm. A finger-post points to Street Gate (which is where the famous old monastic road of Mastiles Lane, on its way from Kilnsey to Malham, becomes a metalled road), and this is the direction to take, but only as far as the fork when you should take the less used track heading SSE. You may then either cut the corner or continue until you intersect with the good track alongside Gordale Beck (grid ref. 912665) and then swing ENE, heading again for the higher land and the return towards Hawkswick. Once again on the plateau, the

*Stone men above
Hawkswick, Littondale*

way becomes rather vague as the track swings off to the north-west, but watch for a finger-post signed 'Arncliffe Cote 2½', pointing north-east. Within minutes, you are passing through a gate in a wall, over the top of the moor and descending towards the grassy hollow where the waters of Cote Gill rise and flow, shadowed by the path, towards Hawkswick.

The observant traveller driving or walking up Littondale and looking to the western skyline above Hawkswick will see a group of typical 'stone men' high on the hillside above. As you ramble down Cote Gill,

you may ponder on the fact that these enigmatic figures, and the fine limestone pavements nearby, though out of sight, are only about a mile north-east of the point at which you begin the descent to Hawkswick; they enjoy superb views over Littondale and as far as Great Whernside.

The track down Cote Gill is a good one, with some attractive views of Littondale and, on reaching the few buildings at Arncliffe Cote, a footpath crosses the road to another pleasant path leading north-westwards alongside the Skirfare and so back to Arncliffe.

40. *The Littondale Skyline*

Best map: OS 1:50,000 Landranger 98 (Wensleydale & Upper Wharfedale). Also on OS 1:25,000 Yorkshire Dales (Western area) & Yorkshire Dales (Northern & Central areas); both will be needed

Distance: About 17 miles/27.2km

Highest elevation reached: 2277ft/694m

Height gained: 1968ft/600m

Overall star rating: **

General level of exertion needed: High

Time for the round: About 8 hours

Terrain: Much of the walk is over rough moor with only sketchy paths.

This splendid round is one of the toughest and longest in this book. It is not nearly so well known as the Three Peaks walk, and will be a bit of a challenge even to regular walkers.

I like to start from Litton – despite the very limited parking there – and, having now done this round four times, I prefer to do it in an anti-clockwise direction which saves the best hill, Pen-y-ghent, until last,

after which it is downhill all the way home. (I have also done it clockwise from Litton, going over Fountains Fell as well as Pen-y-Ghent, but that was piling on the agony a bit.)

There is limited parking on the roadside in Litton near the Queen's Arms (grid ref. 907740), and the bridleway signed for Buckden that gets you out of the valley and on to Old Cote Moor Top starts from beside the pub itself. This leads south-east up a walled lane, crosses Crystal Beck and then soon swings north-east onto open pastures and follows the wall to the top of the fell. Shortly beyond the gate, leave the bridleway and follow the wall along the crest of the broad ridge, passing one or two shallow tarns and a much bigger one, Birks Tarn, on the right. Just north-west of this is a roofless stone building, then the wall swings south around the head of Crystal Beck Gill and the little pap-shape of Sugar Loaf ahead is the target as you tramp over open moor with some evil groughs and bogs to dodge. By-passing Sugar Loaf on your left, the wire fence – which had taken over from the wall – becomes wall again and the trig point of Horse Head is now the objective, over easier ground. The bridleway from Halton Gill to Yockenthwaite is crossed on the way.

Leaving the trig point – which is over the wall – the way now goes west, with fine views up Langstroth-

Towards Littondale from the crags on Pen-y-ghent

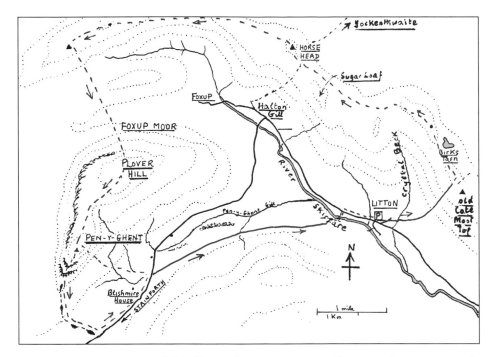

High Greenfield Knott although it is not named as such on the map) is the objective. After this a wall leads down over Foxup Moor towards the watershed between the rivers Skirfare and Ribble; Plover Hill is now directly ahead. It's rough going again descending the fellside; the route passes some shake-holes and a little plantation struggling for life on the watershed, before crossing the Foxup track and tackling the blunt end of Plover Hill. I need my lowest gear on this bit nowadays, but it's soon over and the top of the hill is reached by a stile in a tangle of walls and a finger-post pointing south to the hump of Pen-y-ghent still a mile and a half away. The path is very muddy in places beside the wall but the last pull up to the top should bring a glow of satisfaction. It's now downhill all the way.

On one occasion, I cheated a bit on the way home because I dropped steeply down one of the gullies on the east side of Pen-y-ghent's summit and nipped off down the moor to the east to join the road just to the north of Blishmire House where the finger-post can be seen pointing out the bridleway to Litton. I was glad I had done so because I found a ewe, a young lamb bleating next to it, which had caught its horns firmly between some metal bars across the stream, put there to stop sheep getting out. It lay on its side, gasping, and from the droppings and flattened ground it had been there some considerable time. With difficulty, I was able to release it, and it tottered away with its lamb and, I hope, didn't stick its neck into any more silly places.

dale. For a change, one is walking on limestone and, doing this walk one winter, I found a limestone fossil, an almost perfect impression of a clam shell. The limestone soon disappears, however, and a long decline over brown moor with lumpy grass tufts and groughs follows; this is succeeded by a long ascent towards much greener, higher land and more limestone. Walking over a mainly grass-covered clint-field, the trig point at 1965ft/599m (which is, in fact,

*Towards Litton from
Horse Head Moor*

The official descent is to go south from the summit on the Pennine Way path which you leave when you reach the road. Then you tramp the tarmac for just over a mile until you too reach the bridleway to Litton. Thankfully, this is a pleasant grassy way for nearly all its distance, curving round the fellside until a last descent leads to the valley bottom again, a ramble along the west bank of the Skirfare, which is often dry, and across the final footbridge back to the village.

41.   Buckden Pike via Buckden Beck

Best map: OS 1:25,000 Yorkshire Dales (Northern
    & Central areas)

Distance: About 6½ miles/10.4km

Highest elevation reached: 2303ft/702m

Height gained: 1572ft/479m

Overall star rating: */**

General level of exertion needed: Medium

Time for the round: About 3–4 hours

Terrain: Generally on good paths although with a
    bit of scrambling in the gill.

The usual and more obvious way to climb Buckden Pike is to head north from Buckden up the slanting slope of Buckden Rake and then take a path curving up the northern flank to the top. I think the route I propose is much more interesting and is a splendid way to reach this outstanding viewpoint over Upper Wharfedale, for the lower part of the gill of Buckden Beck is a gem, with delightful waterfalls and amphitheatres.

Buckden is the highest village in the valley and, although quite small, has a large National Park car park which is a very convenient starting point (grid ref. 942775). The gill of Buckden Beck is virtually directly behind the car park and to reach it one just has to turn left (south) from the lower area of the car park until a short walled lane leads to a couple of sheep pens and directly to the bed of the gill. The village draws its water supply from the beck and it hardly needs saying that great care must be taken not to pollute it in any way.

Go straight up the left bank of this delightful ravine, with its white limestone scars rising in tiers, ash trees in profusion and little cascades. One small waterfall is followed by another about twenty feet high set in a small amphitheatre; this looks like an impasse, but a ledge slanting back left soon leads to a higher level. In a hundred paces there is another, longer cascade and amphitheatre, passed by on the left like the first. Immediately above is yet a third waterfall and amphitheatre, and this time an easy if steep little scramble (good holds) just to the left of the cascade gets you over the lip without having to go dodging off to the side, although you could do so if necessary. Several more smaller waterfalls occur higher up which are easily passed by on the right.

Then the beck suddenly comes to an end where it wells forth just beyond the end of a large spoil-heap and ruined mine building, whose stone-arched tunnel

*The Walden Road
leading into Starbotton*

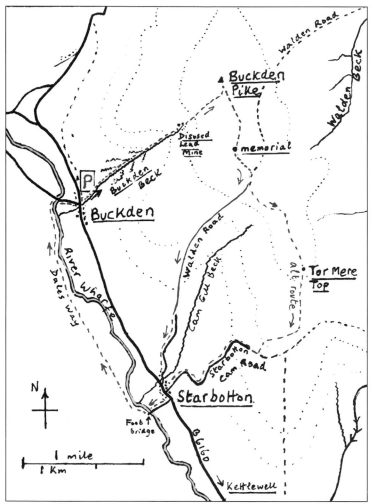

is seen once you are above the spoil. There is now a faint path up gritstone moorland to the summit ridge, bearing left (north-east) to reach the stone wall and the trig point on Buckden Pike just beyond. From here there are splendid views in most directions, particularly down Waldendale to the north-east, as far as Penhill overlooking Wensleydale and with a grand prospect over upper Wharfedale.

Going south now along the summit ridge can be a soggy business as the top of the moor is fairly level and much of the peat has been churned into a glutinous mud, but it isn't long before you reach the memorial cross erected to the Polish airmen who crashed near here in January 1942. I once found bits of aeroplane wreckage high on Whernside Pasture nearly eight miles away and often wonder whether it came from the Polish plane.

There's now a slight descent alongside the wall to a boundary stone and a right-angle corner in the wall with a gate. The old packhorse trail of the Walden Road passes through this, linking Wharfedale with Waldendale, and you now have a choice of either turning down it or continuing along the line of the ridge: in the latter case, you stay alongside the summit wall until you reach Tor Mere Top. Continuing that way is a straightforward tramp slightly down and then up again, followed by a simple descent down to the Starbotton Cam Road, the lower part of which is down an old walled lane.

The Walden Road descent, however, is less enclosed and follows a very pleasant green way on the

Buckden Beck

open slopes above the Cam Gill Beck, giving a classic Wharfedale view of enclosed fields, green valley bottom and steep-sided fell as you approach the village of Starbotton.

Leave the village going south on the Kettlewell road to find the finger-post and the little walled lane leading to the footbridge and ford over the Wharfe.

The Dales Way is joined here, giving a delightful stroll back along the level valley floor on the western side of the river, partly along its bank, partly down narrow lanes but there are plenty of finger-posts and signs to ensure that you reach Buckden Bridge. Turn right over the bridge and make your way back into the village.

189

42. The Head of Wharfedale

Best map: OS 1:25,000 Yorkshire Dales (Northern & Central areas plus Western area). Except for the last 2 miles, the walk is well-signed along the Dales Way and the OS 1:50,000 Landranger 98 (Wensleydale & Upper Wharfedale) covers it all

Distance: About 11½ miles/18.4km

Highest elevation reached: 1903ft/580m

Height gained: 1171ft/357m

Overall star rating: * * *

General level of exertion needed: Medium

Time for the walk: About 5–6 hours

Terrain: Good paths or tracks but rough moor (downhill) when the end in sight.

This walk, from Buckden to Newby Head Moss, is *not* a round; transport needs to be planned so that you can be collected from Newby Head, unless two parties meet half way and exchange car keys, but it is unquestionably worth making the effort to enjoy this superb walk up the headwaters of one of England's loveliest rivers. The valley landscape through which it alternately rushes and winds is one of ever-changing variety, with dark brown gritstone moors, woodlands, startling white limestone crags and silver-grey walls enclosing bright green fields. The walk is magical in late spring when birdsong enhances the scenery.

A start could be made in Starbotton, adding about 2½ miles/4km to the walk, but parking is very difficult there, whereas there is a large National Park car park in Buckden (grid ref. 942775). Leaving this, simply cross Buckden Bridge to the west bank of the Wharfe and a gate leads to the path alongside the river, shadowing it for a little way until it joins the narrow road (Dubb's Lane) on the approach to Hubberholme. This delightful hamlet, consisting of little more than a farm, the homely and well-loved George Inn, and a bridge connecting it to the ancient church of St Michael (the pub was once the vicarage) is where the Dales Way crosses the river to the north bank.

It is certainly well worth looking into the church with its great timber-beamed roof with leaded exterior, rough stone arches dating back to the twelfth century and its famous oak rood loft; here the musicians sat before the days of the church organ and this one is a rare survivor since they were nearly all destroyed during Puritan times. We have an oak coffee-table at home which has a little mouse carved in the wood running up one of the legs, the trademark

Upper Wharfedale approaching Beckermonds

of its maker, Robert Thompson of Kilburn. I was delighted to spot lots of the same little mice running up the ends of the pews in this church.

There are two routes between the hamlets of Hubberholme and Yockenthwaite. Both start by going through a gate to the right of the church and passing behind it. Then one route makes the short climb to the early Quaker meeting-place of Scar House which allows a traverse at a higher level to Yockenthwaite.

The more usual route, our friend the Dales Way, stays close to the north bank – in fact, Wharfedale has now become Langstrothdale – by the edges of Raise Wood and Strans Wood. Here the river flows over grooved limestone slabs and the path passes through delightful traditional hay meadows full of flowers in June. Near Yockenthwaite, the narrow road on the other bank is much closer to the river and is unfenced so that it forms a delightful stretch for the occasional picnicking motorist. The Dales Way keeps to the

north bank and doesn't cross the bridge here. Instead, it passes a modest stone circle and reaches the next little farming settlement at Deepdale before exchanging banks with the road at Deepdale Bridge.

A broad path over limestone slabs between the river and a wall now leads towards the confluence of Green Field Beck and the Wharfe and, after passing some little waterfalls, reaches the next hamlet at Beckermonds where a footbridge leads to a right turn back to the valley road. The next bit, to Oughtershaw, is a tramp up a steep bit of road that can't be avoided, but at least it is away from the conifer forest up Green Field Beck, and welcome refreshment is usually available in Oughtershaw.

Leaving the hamlet and the road, a signed track goes up the now broad and open valley towards the headwaters of Oughtershaw Beck and stays firm underfoot past the farm at Nethergill as far as the farm at Swarthgill, with wide-ranging views back towards Wharfedale. From here on is sterner stuff with a

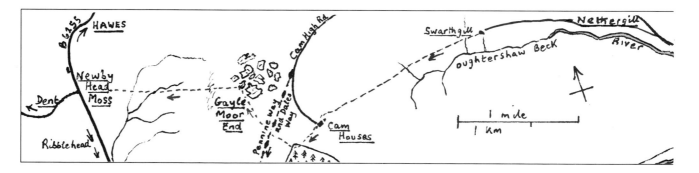

rougher path climbing towards the cluster of buildings seen ahead at Cam Houses. Beyond these, the path leads ahead to cut through the corner of a conifer plantation by a couple of stiles, crossing a forestry track and continuing to climb to a finger-post and cairn where the Dales Way joins the Pennine Way on the old Roman Cam High Road on its long march from Bainbridge to Ingleton.

From here the Dales Way takes a little over five miles to the next point, but as the crow flies – and you can walk – it's only two miles to Newby Head Moss and the junction of the Dentdale road with that going to Hawes (at grid ref. 795836) which is a much more certain location for your patient driver anyway. All you have to do is climb a little further to the north up onto the clints of Gayle End Moor. From here the buildings of Newby Head Farm should be visible to the north-west and, with luck, your transport will be there too. All that remains is a stretch of rough but exhilarating moorland as the end to a splendid walk.

Herding sheep in Langstrothdale

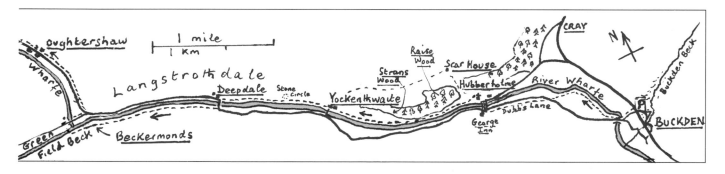

43. Over Old Cote Moor

Best map: OS 1:50,000 Landranger 98 (Wensleydale & Upper Wharfedale).
If you use the 1:25,000 maps, you need both Northern & Central and Southern areas

Distance: About 8½ miles/13.6km for the 'low road'; 6¾ miles/10.8km for the 'high road'

Highest elevation reached: 1706ft/520m

Height gained: 1772ft/540m (you climb up twice); or 1854ft/565m

Overall star rating: **

General level of exertion needed: Medium

Time for the round: About 4 hours or 3½ hours for the shorter walk

Terrain: Generally good paths throughout.

The rivers Wharfe and Skirfare are separated by Old Cote Moor whose blunt prow of Knipe Scar is well seen from the east side of Wharfedale. This walk does a double crossing of the moor, and the sharp contrast between the dark gritstone moors and the green limestone pastures of the valleys, with the walls and barns which make the Dales scenery so distinctive, is particularly striking as a result. Don't start too early in the day for if ever a walk was suited to a lunchtime picnic or pub lunch, this is it – although the time given for these two alternative walks does not assume that two hours are spent gargling the lotion in Arncliffe!

Start from the National Park car park just over the river bridge in Kettlewell (grid ref. 967723) – from where sometimes you may also be able to watch a hot-air balloon being launched from the other bank – then decide whether you are going to take the 'low road' to Hawkswick or the ultimately shorter 'high road' direct to Arncliffe.

If you choose the latter, cross back over the Wharfe and turn right immediately through the gate when a path (with a finger-post sign for Arncliffe) slants steeply up the hillside to a little gully in the limestone scar. From the top there are delightful views northwards up Wharfedale and back to Kettlewell. The path now leads up the moor, a little vaguely in places, over ladder-stiles to the wall on the top; then a slanting descent follows towards the attractive village of Arncliffe, soon seen coming into view at the junction of the Cowside Beck and the Skirfare. The last stage is a sharp descent of Park Scar and through the fine ash trees of Byre Bank Wood, with a last easy bit down sheep pasture to the village.

Kettlewell and Great Whernside from the edge of Old Cote Moor

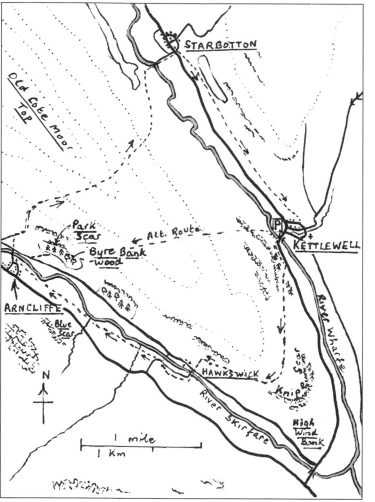

If you opt to go first to Hawkswick, which is a slightly longer route but perhaps more attractive, you must cross the river in Kettlewell but then walk back south beside the road for about three hundred yards to where there is a sign by a gate: 'FP Hawkswick 2M'. A path, initially quite rocky, slants up through a mixed wood of ash and sycamore then through the corner of a conifer plantation and via a couple of stiles to a delightful green way climbing gently below a line of shattered scars and on to a shelf, from where it curves round above Knipe Scar to a stile on the top of the moor. The pastures below Knipe Scar are called High Wind Bank and are popular for picnics on warm summer days; they are also used for training novice hang-gliders.

On one visit I watched two advanced students, with their lady instructor, toil up to near the top of the moor instead of staying on the lower slopes. They kept waiting for the wind conditions to be just right and unwittingly gave the local farmer enough time to come puffing up to tell them that they weren't allowed to fly from there. He also gave me a wigging for straying about ten yards off the path while I was watching them but I made sure I did stay long enough to see them eventually take off and go soaring down Littondale towards the great overhang of Kilnsey Crag.

The path slants down sharply to Hawkswick, a pleasing collection of mellow stone houses and farm buildings beside the Skirfare which is spanned by an old bridge. Either turn right through the village and

Arncliffe church and the River Skirfare

over the footbridge, or cross the main bridge and wander along until a narrow ginnel leads to the same footbridge. Here a path leads up the west side of the tree-lined river bank, through meadows and below the vertical limestone walls of Blue Scar, into Arncliffe with its riverside church, village green and pub.

Whether you reach Arncliffe by the longer route through Hawkswick or come directly over the moor from Kettlewell, the route back is the same. To leave, go over the river bridge, to the junction of the main road down the valley with the single-track road on the east bank which leads back to Hawkswick. Here a finger-post points you over the wall and steeply up the field via a couple of stiles to join a farm track winding up onto the moor again. You'll reach a line of shake-holes, then pass a lonely hut up on the heather-covered gritstone moor before crossing again for fine views of Great Whernside and the southern slopes of Buckden Pike. The well-cairned path now leads gently down until a steeper descent leads to a foot-bridge and walled lane to Starbotton.

Cross the road and on the other side find a path signed for Kettlewell; this last couple of miles on the sunny side of the Wharfe is a delightful day.

197

44. Great Whernside and Dowber Gill

Best map: OS 1:25,000 Yorkshire Dales (Northern & Central areas)

Distance: About 8½ miles/13.6km. Add 1 mile/1.6 km to go to Tor Mere Top

Highest elevation reached: 2310ft/704m

Height gained: 1624ft/495m. Add 410ft/125m to go to Tor Mere Top

Overall star rating: */**

General level of exertion needed: Medium/high

Time for the round: About 4–5 hours

Terrain: A fair path up Dowber Gill Beck, rough moor over Great Whernside, then good tracks back to the valley.

Arguably the best high-level fell walk in Wharfedale is the traverse of the eastern skyline from Great Whernside to Buckden Pike, but you need to arrange return transport or hike the four miles along the Dales Way. This proposed walk doesn't go quite so far as Buckden Pike but, as a result, allows a direct return and a good round.

There is a large car park in Kettlewell just over the river bridge (grid ref. 967723), then, walking towards the village, veer to the right (south-east) on the minor road which leads to Conistone and Grassington. In a couple of hundred yards, turn left where the road is signed for Leyburn, pass the King's Head pub on the left and then keep straight on up a narrow lane ('Police' sign on the wall) with Dowber Gill Beck on the left. Ignore the finger-post for Whernside Pasture and keep to the right bank of the beck. Then, before the junction with Cam Gill Beck, fork right and cross the beck by a shallow ford to where there's a finger-post for Hag Dike and Providence Pot. You don't want the path for Hag Dike, formerly a marginal farm but now an outdoor centre, but the other which leads roughly east up the limestone gill which is initially wooded. You soon pass a pretty little four-tier waterfall and then head for the dark gritstone moorland and a line of cairns on the skyline. A little further up the gill, yet higher moorland is seen beyond a gritstone boulder slope. Providence Pot, originally below a slit in the stream-bed but now with a square concrete manhole, which is the beginning of a classic underground journey of nearly a mile, is reached at a fork in the gill; a little higher, above the right-hand beck (Dowber Gill Wham), are the spoil-heaps of the former Providence lead-mine.

Keep going up this pathless right-hand gill now,

Dowber Gill and Great Whernside seen from the Coverdale road

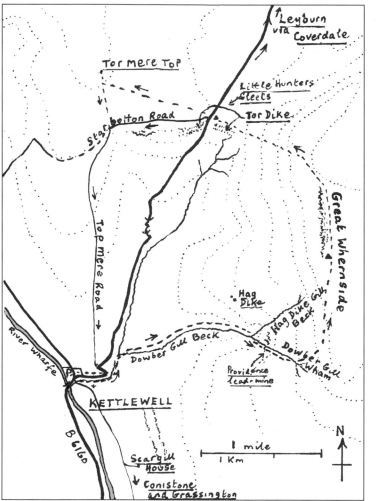

and you soon climb above the limestone level. As the gill fades into moorland, there is a cluster of sheep-folds and a line of stone men just beyond to the south-west. Ahead now lies wild moor, rising in a long slope with a final steeper upward curve on to a broad ridge of peat hags, heather and crumbling gritstone. From here are tremendous views down the head of Nidderdale to the great Angram and Scar House Reservoirs. Now you must veer to the north, towards the line of strangely square gritstone boulders, where the OS column will be found amongst a jumble of them; just a little further north is a splendid circular stone shelter which is a better place to stop.

On leaving, continue to more scattered stones and then go gently downhill to the north-north-west. As I left the summit, on my last visit the wind rolled a grey mist towards me and I was soon in pouring rain as well but still had no problem finding the wall junction which is reached just where the ridge begins to curve to the north-east towards Little Whernside. Turn downhill due west beside the wall, then over a stile and to the north-west on a steep path which leads quickly across the flank of Great Whernside to reach the Coverdale road at its highest point, Little Hunters Sleets. Just before you reach the road, you should be able to see clearly the remains of the ditch and earthworks of Tor Dike which were erected by the Brigantes nearly two thousand years ago to keep the Romans in the south – which it failed to do.

On a fine day, you may choose to extend the walk from here to take in Tor Mere Top, the next high

Looking north along the top of Great Whernside to Tor Dike

point along the Wharfedale skyline but really just a lump on the ridge where peat used to be cut for Kettlewell. It's a simple but soggy walk heading north-west over a couple of stiles to reach the high point and a fine view. The descent involves going southwards alongside the wall until a ladder-stile leads to the junction of the tracks named on the map as 'Starbotton Road' and 'Top Mere Road'.

If you don't go to Tor Mere Top, you head south-west from the highest point of the road along a track alongside another bit of Tor Dike; this almost immediately joins the Starbotton Road and the junc-tion with the Top Mere Road. Kettlewell is signed from here, along a green way, becoming a walled lane (Top Mere Road); this descends to meet the Cover-dale road on a bend just out of the village.

I was still soaking wet when I reached the car park and so got out my bit of carpet to stand on. A large party of Ramblers' Association members, who had also been out for a tramp, were decorously getting out of their wet things: they gave me some old-fashioned looks as I stripped off to my underpants before pulling some dry clothes on. I expect I deserved the looks – I don't suppose it was a pretty sight.

45.　How Stean Gorge and the Head of Nidderdale

Best map:　OS 1:25,000 Yorkshire Dales (Northern & Central areas)

Distance:　About 10 miles/16km

Highest elevation reached:　1424ft/434m

Height gained:　768ft/234m

Overall star rating:　**/***

General level of exertion needed:　Medium

Time for the round:　About 5 hours

Terrain:　Mostly on fair to good paths, some of which are wet on the high land.

How Stean Gorge is a treat in itself, and the walk described is very good and with splendid views, far better than I ever expected.

The usual approach is from Pateley Bridge to Lofthouse from where there are signs for How Stean Gorge. Park in the car park by the excellent café (near the spot marked Cat Hole on the OS map, grid ref. 094735). You'll have to pay to enter the gorge but it is very definitely worth visiting: deep and narrow with marvellous sculpting of the rock, protected pathways along overhung ledges, little footbridges and even a trip of nearly two hundred yards through the passages of Tom Tinker's Cave.

Leaving the gorge, turn right (north) up the road towards Stean village but, just before reaching it, take the path signed for Middlesmoor and 'Nidderdale Way', re-crossing the gorge by a footbridge. Climb the short steep bank on the other side but then turn sharp left (north-west) through a slit-stile and then over a large ladder-stile just beyond. A path now leads through a lightly wooded area along the bank of the How Stean Beck until it enters a little wood with an open glade in its middle. Just beyond this, opposite two little waterfalls, the path climbs back uphill again to a stile and yellow arrow.

Here is a junction of paths and it is a crucial point. Continue along the main path for only fifty paces or so beyond the stile (after which the main path starts to descend again) and look for another stile almost hidden by the side of the wall. Pass through this and continue on a slightly rising and less-used path which leads north-westwards, with more yellow marker arrows, to pass the derelict farm at Ruscoe, then across more pasture to the occupied farm buildings of Intake Farm. Climb gently (no path) to the north-west across the field beyond and to a gate in a wall. Continue to another, with a cattle-grid, where the farm track is joined. Just ahead along the track is

Looking down Upper Nidderdale from near Scar House

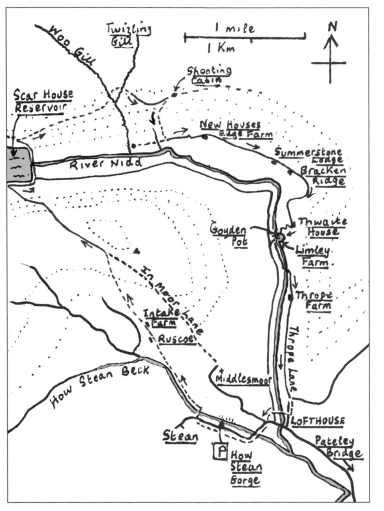

another gate and cattle-grid but turn off on a good track to the right (north) just before reaching it, climbing up the moor to reach the walled In Moor Lane. Continue along this now, with miles of rolling grouse moor laid out before you, until a panoramic view of Scar House Reservoir is seen below.

The track zigzags down below frowning gritstone crags to reach the reservoir, and a right turn leads you to the road across the top of the dam itself and a spectacular view to the waterslide and down Nidderdale.

On the far side of the dam, turn left up a track then back right, to the ENE, (sign 'Nidderdale Way') on a boggy path rising across moorland. It then descends a little to cross the stream in the eroded Woo Gill and then that in Twizling Gill. Climbing out of the latter, the path, now a substantial track, continues slanting across bracken-covered moor until ahead can be seen a flat-topped concrete shooting-cabin. Just before reaching it, a line of white-topped posts marks a rough track which slants down across the fellside to a gate in a wall. Go through this, turn right and downhill, then swing left and through a couple of gates to reach a more substantial track on the level and another sign for 'Nidderdale Way'. Turn left (east) here and follow this good, grassy track until it forks. Don't descend towards the river, but take the left fork leading slightly uphill to cross a little gill and reach New Houses Edge Farm. The good track continues to Bracken Ridge Farm then swings south, shadowing the curve of the river in the valley below and with some fine views. At Thwaite House, it zigzags steeply downhill towards the valley bottom but swings left before reaching the river towards a large barn.

The River Nidd in this area flows along at several different levels. The main flow sinks at Manchester Hole about three hundred yards upstream from here. Any overflow continues until it reaches a jutting limestone scar where it too disappears into a slit at its base. This is Goyden Pot, and you may inspect it yourself if you leave the track on the last bend, before reaching the barn, and continue down the rest of the field, across two collapsed walls, to reach the river bed. It is dangerous to enter the pot if any water is flowing. All the waters that sink reappear at Nidd Heads which lies about two miles downstream near Lofthouse.

Retrace your steps to the track, pass the barn and follow the path (arrows) across the dry river bed and up through the buildings of Limley Farm which are perched on the oxbow bend. The signs then lead alongside the river bank again, to re-cross shortly later at Dry Wath (ford). From here the path leads away from the river, joins a walled lane and reaches Thrope Farm beyond which Thrope Lane gives a most delightful ramble down the valley to reach the tarmac just outside Lofthouse. Turn right down a ginnel immediately past the war memorial/fountain, re-cross the river by the bridge and cross the dam access road to a path opposite, signed for Middlesmoor. In a hundred yards you'll see the signs again for How Stean Gorge and the car park is just up the road.

How Stean Gorge

Index

Addlebrough   130, 133–5, *135*
Aisgill Moor Cottages   105, 111, 116
Alum Pot   54–5
Arant Haw   91, 92
Arncliffe   *178,* 179, 195, 197, *197*
Askrigg   137
Attermire Scar & Cave   18–19
Austwick   21
Aye Gill Pike   50
Aysgarth Falls   *120,* 121
Aysgarth Templars' Chapel   121

Barbondale   41, 43
Bardale   131
Barden Fell   159
Barden Moor   163–5
Baugh Fell   50, 79, 86, 87–9, 112, 113
Beckermonds   *190,* 192
Beezley Falls, Ingleton   31
Beggarman's Road   131, *131*
Beldi Hill & Mine   8, 146
Ben End   79, 81
Birkwith Gill & Cave   53, 64
Black Force   95, 96, 97, 100
Blakethwaite Bottom   97, 100
Blind Gill, Swaledale   150, 151
Bolton Abbey   159
Bowderdale   79, 83, 101

Brackenbottom   57, 64
Bram Rigg Top   84, 91, 92
Breaks Head   97, 100
Buck Haw Brow   70
Buckden Beck   187, *189*
Buckden Pike   125, 187–9, 199
Bunton Mine, Swaledale   *148,* 150
Burnsall   167
Butter Tubs Pass   142

Calders   84, 91, 92
Calf, The   84, 91, 92, 93, 97, 99, 100–1
Cam High Road   129, *129,* 130–1, *131,* 193
Carlin Gill   93, 95–7, 99, 100
Carlow Stone   129
Catrigg Force   17–18
Cautley Crag & Spout   76, 79, 83–5, 112
Celtic Wall   69
Chapel-le-Dale   61
Chapel Beck   91, 93, 97
Cheese Press Stone, Kingsdale   39
Clapdale   25
Clapham   25
Clough Force   115
Coast to Coast Walk   108, 109
Coldbergh Edge   *106,* 108
Conistone Pie   177, *177*
Cote Gill   181

Coverdale   *123*
Cow Hole (Cow Dubbs)   43
Cowgill   50
Crackpot Hall, Swaledale   146
Crag Hill   43
Craven Way   47, 65
Crina Bottom   33, 35
Crookrise Crag   163–4
Crummackdale   21–3

Dales Way   47, 51, 161, 167, 175, 189, 191, 192–3
Deepdale   *44,* 46–7
Deer Gallows Ridge   *162,* 164
Dent   45, 47, 49
Dentdale   49–51
Devil's Stone, Addlebrough   129, 134–5
Doe, river   31
Drumaldrace   130

Ease Gill   41–2, *43*
Eden, river   103, 104, 116
Ellerkin Scar   *137,* 138
Embsay Crag   163, 165
Embsay Moor   *162*
Embsay Moor Reservoir   163, *165*
Ewes Top   30, 37

Feizor   69–70
Fell Head   91, 93, 95, 97
Flinter Gill   45
Fossdale   142, *143*
Fountains Fell   74–5
Foxup Moor   58, 184

Gaisgill   99
Gaping Gill   *24*, 25, 26
Garsdale   *48*, 49, 50
Garsdale Head   113, 117
Gibbet Hill, Howgills   95
Giggleswick Scar   68, 70
Gordale Scar   155, 156, 157, *157*
Gragareth   *11*, *35*, 37, 38
Grassington   175
Great Agill Beck   160
Great Coum   43
Great Dummacks   84
Great Douk Cave   67
Great Shunner Fell   *141*, 141–3
Great Whernside   125, *152*, *194*, 197, *198*,
   199–200, *201*
Greensett Tarn   65
Grisedale   *114*, 115–17
Gunnerside   149
Gunnerside Gill   *148*, 149–50, *151*

Halton Height   165
Hanging Lund   113
Hangingstone Scar   103, 105
Hardraw Force   141
Harland Hill   *124*
Hawes   141

Hawkswick   181, *181*, 196, 197
Hebden Gill   9, *170*, 171
Hell Gill   104, 105, 116
Hell Gill Force   116, *117*
High Clint   *141*, 142
High Pike Hill   103
High Seat   *105*
High Way, The   104, 105, 116–17
High White Scar   112
Horse Head   183
Horton in Ribblesdale   53, 57
How Stean Gorge   203, 205
Howgill Lane (Wharfedale)   159, 160–1
Hubberholme   191
Hugh Seat   103–4, 105
Hull Pot & Beck   57, 58–9, 64
Humphrey Bottom   34, 67

Ingleborough   *24*, 25–7, *32*, 33–5, 66, 67,
   134
Ingleborough Cave   25
Ingleborough Hall   25, 27
Ingleton Glens   29–31

Janet's Foss   155, 156
Jingling Pot   38
Juniper Cave & Gulf   26

Kail Hill   167, 169
Kensgriff   79
Kettlewell   *194*, 195, 199, 201
Kingsdale   *11*, *36*, 37–9
Kinsey Cave   70
Kirkby Gate   30, 37, 67

Kisdon   *118*, 145
Kisdon Force   145, *147*
Knipe Scar   *174*, 177, 195, 196
Knoutberry Haw   89

Lamps Moss   107, 109
Langcliffe   17
Langcliffe Mill   71
Langdale   99–101
Langstrothdale   183, 192, *193*
Little Fell   105
Long Churn Caves   54–5
Low Ash Gill Woods   131

Malham Cove   *154*, 155–7
Malham Tarn   73–4, 157, 180
Mallerstang   103–5
Megger Stones   45
Meregill Hole   34
Middle House   73, 179–80
Mill Gill Force   137, *138*
Monk's Road   73, 179–81
Moughton   22, *23*

Nab, The   112–13
Newby Head   191, 193
Ney Gill   108
Nine Standards   107–9
Norber   20, *21*

Occupation Road   38, 43, *44*, 45–6
Old Cote Moor   183, 195–7
Oughtershaw   192
Oxford Pot   43

Pecca Falls   29, *31*
Pendragon Castle   *102*, 104–5
Penhill   121–3, 125, 134
Pennine Way   53, 59, 64, 74–5, 141, 145–6, 155
Pen-y-ghent   *23*, 53, 57–9, 60, 64, *73*, 75, *105*, 183, 184
Pen-y-ghent Café, Horton   61–2, *63*
Pike Hill   141–2
Plover Hill   57, 58, 184
Posforth Gill & Force   159–60, *161*
Pot Scar   *14*, 69
Providence Pot   199

Randygill Top,   80
Raven Scar   34–5
Raven Ray   30
Ravenseat   108, 109
Rawthey, river   79, 83–4, 87–8
Ribblehead viaduct   34, 65
Rise Hill   49–51
Rispa Pike   100
Robin Proctor's Scar   21
Rogan's Seat   151
Rollinson Haggs   108
Rowten Pot   39
Rylstone Cross   164, 165

Scale Force   9, 171
Scar House Reservoir   200, 204
Seat Knott   91
Sedbusk   143
Sell Gill Holes   53
Selside   54

Semer Water   129, 130
Settle   17
Settle-Carlisle Railway   50, 111, 115, 116
Simon Fell   26, 67
Simon's Seat   *158*, 159, 160
Sir Francis Mine, Swaledale   149, *151*
Skirfare river   184, 185, 195, 196–7, *197*
Smearsett Scar   *14*, 69, *70*
Snaizewold Fell   50
Snow Falls, Ingleton   31
Stackhouse   70–1
Stags Fell   141, 142, *143*
Stainforth   69
Stainforth Force   71
Street, The   87, 89
Strid, The   161
Sulber Gate   22
Sulber Nick   55, 67
Swale Gorge   8, 145–7
Swarth Fell   79, 88, 105, 110, 111–13, 115
Swarth Gill Gate   58, 64
Swarth Greaves Beck   92
Swilla Gill   29
Swinden Quarry   164
Swinner Gill   *144*, 145–7, 151

Taythes Gill   89
Thornton Force   *28*, 29–30
Thornton Rusk   133
Three Peaks Walk   34, 37, 55, 61–7
Thupton Gill   122, 125, *127*
Thwaite   *118*, 145, 147
Tor Mere Top   200–1
Trollers Gill   167, 168, *169*

Trow Gill   25–6
Turbary Road   38–9
Twisleton Lane   30, 31, 37
Twisleton Scars   *11*, 31, *35*
Twiss, river   29

Uldale Beck   97, 100
Uldale Force   88, 89
Uldale Head   97, 100
Ulgill Beck   94, 96, 97, 98, 100

Victoria Cave, Settle   18

Walden Beck   123
Waldendale   125–6, 188
Wandale Hill   79, 80, *81*
Waterfall Gill   164, 165
West Burton   123
Westerdale   81
Wether Hill   130, 131
Whernside   *27*, 36, 37, 45–7, 65–7, *105*
Whin Stone Gill   87
White Fell Head   91, 93, 100
Whitfield Gill & Force   137, 138
Whitsundale   108, 109
Wild Boar Fell   58, 79, 105, 111–13, *113*
Wind Scarth   100
Winskill   *14* , 17
Woodhall   139

Yarlside   79
Yockenthwaite   *3*, 193
Yordas Cave   38